Epworth Mechanics' Institute Library
Tuesday 10a.m – 12 Noon
Thursday 1.30p.m – 4p.m
Friday 7.30p.m – 9.30p.m

14·5·15

S

D1513292

**Please return books as soon as you have finished with
them so that others may read them**

BARRIE PEPPER

THE LANDLORD'S TALE

Author: Barrie Pepper

Illustrations by Christine Jopling
Cover photography: Barrie Pepper
Cover design by Rob Howells
Printed by Budget Book Manufacturing

Published by CAMRA, The Campaign for Real Ale, 230 Hatfield Road, St. Albans, Herts AL1 4LW

Managing Editor: Mark Webb, mark-webb@msn. com

© CAMRA Ltd 2002

ISBN 1-85249-171-X

Conditions of Sale:
This book shall not, by way of trade or otherwise, be lent, resold, hired out or otherwise circulated without the publisher's prior consent in any form of binding or cover other than in which it is published and without similar conditions being imposed on the subsequent purchaser. All rights reserved. No parts of this publication may be reproduced, stored in retrieval systems, or transmitted in any form or by any means electronic, mechanical, photocopying or otherwise, without the prior permission of CAMRA Limited.

CONTENTS

FOREWORD

YOU MAY WONDER WHAT A TEETOTALLER – if only for the past six years – is doing writing a foreword to this book about life in and around a 1950s industrial West Riding pub. You will be mystified when I tell you that I avoid pubs because I have lost my anonymity after 10 years on TV and some people seem to regard me as a satisfactory substitute for telling Margaret Thatcher what they think of her. I was her chief press secretary. I regard the word "spindoctor" as a term of abuse.

The answer to the conundrum is that I know Wilf Lowe from a long way back when we were aspiring young Fabians in Leeds and I seem to recognise the Coach and Four in Oldford and Calderthorpe up the hill. Indeed, I rather think I covered Calderthorpe Rugby League Club for the Yorkshire Evening Post and Yorkshire Post for 10 years. It is almost inevitable that I also reported Wilf's father's licensing extension applications at the West Riding Court in Calderthorpe since I went there every day it sat for a good six years.

As you read these pages you will recognise Keith Waterhouse's fictional – but only too real – Clogthorpe and its civic affairs which he chronicles in the *Daily Mail*. Certainly, there is nothing in this book that will come as a surprise to Mr Waterhouse. It is the authentic drinking man's West Riding of the 1950s. Wilf Lowe, the publican's son, captures beautifully a past all us pensioners recognise from the brewery dray horses, one of which sadly expires climbing the hill to Calderthorpe, to the interminable verbosity of the chosen many to speak at the annual dinner of the Licensed Victuallers' Association.

His account also fills me with envy. If only I could have attended the Coach and Four's unique rendering of Handel's 'Messiah'. There is an entire TV episode waiting to be made of this vignette. I speak as an authority, having once played second cornet in Hebden Bridge Brass Band and second violin in Todmorden Orchestra, both up the valley from Oldford, I suspect, and, as a youth, pumped the organ for 'The Messiah' at Hope

4

Baptist Chapel in Hebden Bridge after the 1946 floods had wrecked its electric motor which drove the bellows.

It is perfectly clear to me that Wilf Lowe missed his calling. He should have been an impresario which is what, incidentally, publican's used to be, as you will discover.

As the old News of the World advert on a hoarding in Armley, Leeds, put it "All human life is there." It certainly is in Wilf Lowe's Coach and Four. This is a very human tale – and entirely credible.

Bernard Ingham

THANKS

THANKS ARE DUE TO A LOT of people but in particular to my late parents Elsie and Alex Pepper who ran a good pub and formed many friendships in doing so. I never really believed all the tales my father told me but I always enjoyed them and I'm sure he's still telling them while pulling pints of Holy Ale in that big taproom in the sky with my mum alongside making well-filled sandwiches for the angelic punters. My greatest regret is that dad missed out on 1997 which saw the return of a Labour government, his grandson's graduation and Barnsley gaining promotion to soccer's top division.

Thanks also go to my dear wife Carolynne who encouraged me to carry on when the publisher who gave me a verbal commission backed out. I got the same support from my daughter Yvette and from Ted Bruning. It was Ted's idea that it would be a better book if it was illustrated and I have Christine Jopling to thank for the pictures. For the foreword I thank Bernard Ingham – he is a colleague from way back who knows the area well and probably drank in the Coach and Four if he did but know it. And finally, and as ever, thanks to Howard Bicknell for reading and editing the script and giving me the benefit of his experience.

Barrie Pepper

INTRODUCTION AND DEDICATION

"It's the fourth leg of the table that causes the wobble."
TAPROOM PHILOSOPHY FROM BARRIE PEPPER

IT WAS NOT EASY RUNNING A PUB in the nineteen-fifties but at least you knew whom you were running it for. Most of the owners were also the brewers, and both managers and tenants had a relationship with them that was generally straightforward and patently honest. There were some bad employers, there was some poor beer and there were some awful landlords but, on the whole, drinkers knew what they wanted and usually got it – or they went elsewhere.

It was with this background that my parents moved from the Lancashire coast, where my father was the steward of an employees' sports club, to a tenancy with a regional brewery in the West Riding of Yorkshire – his home county. It was their first pub and they stayed five years before moving on to their own free house.

This is their story of that period told in the words of my alter ego Wilf Lowe. Their life was not all beer and skittles – there was plenty of humdrum hard work – and not all that is recounted here happened to them, but this is made clear. However, the tale attempts to portray pub life in the fifties – the days when it seemed to me that beer tasted better than it does today, accountants were there to pay the bills and kept their noses out of the gentle art of making beer, brewers were held in high esteem and keg beer was practically unheard of.

Licensees are a much maligned lot and some deserve the brickbats they get but most of them do a fine job and give a great deal of pleasure by providing as they do a unique public service.

This book is dedicated to landlords and landladies everywhere.

Barrie Pepper

CHAPTER 1

....

THE PROLOGUE – MOVING IN

"The rooms and stables of the inn were wide;
They made us easy, all was of the best."
THE CANTERBURY TALES – CHAUCER,

TEN O' CLOCK ON A MONDAY MORNING seemed to me rather a daft time to take over a pub. But, the brewery assured us, it was the time it was always done. How then, I queried, poking my nose in, did the chap going out and moving to another pub manage to be at both places at the same time? There was no answer but the look on my father's face was enough to tell me to shut up.

The outgoing landlord, a man called Titchener, was chisel-faced and wore a shiny suit. His mouth curved into a droopy sort of sneer under his thin moustache and he wore a military looking tie of questionable origin. His wife had a built-in snarl and an 'I've-got-you-summed-up' expression. Without question she knew the wages of all her customers to the last penny. If she had kept a seaside boarding house she would have charged for the use of the cruet.

The stocktaking was completed and I was glad to see this unhappy couple depart. When I discovered where they were moving to I marked it down as a pub to avoid. I wondered if my parents would develop into this sort of couple. Was it the licensee syndrome? Could you identify them from other folk as you could, for example, pick out horsy types by their lack of chins, spiked noses and rather daft headgear? I hoped not.

However, the formalities had taken thirty minutes and the pub had to open on time at eleven o' clock. My presence there was to lend a hand. Or so my father said. I had never pulled a pint in my life so I lit a cigarette and was about to test my skills – or lack of them. This was my first mistake. My mother, who was normally never seen without a fag in her mouth, had learned her lessons well. 'Put that cigarette out,' she bawled at me, 'and never let me see you smoking behind that bar again!'

I too was learning fast. Pulling pints was no easy job, particularly in this part of Yorkshire where they wanted a tight head on their beer. And what about prices? I was a teacher of English and history, not mathematics and, not to put too fine a point on it, practically innumerate. But the pub had to open on time.

My father had taken over the tenancy of the Coach and Four at Oldford in the West Riding of Yorkshire. Our family had a Yorkshire background – father, mother and I had all been born there – so our 20 year sojourn in Lancashire, where my two sisters were born and where the old man had been a club steward for some time, we hoped would not be held against us.

Oldford had been built about a year before town planning was discovered. It was a product of the industrial revolution that had been grafted on to an existing, tiny medieval village of a church, four pubs and a clutch of houses around a green. Progress in the shape of a trunk road had done for the green and only the church and two of the pubs remained, one of which was ours.

'The Coach', as everybody seemed to call it, was a large eighteenth-century coaching inn that had gone through some rebuilding around 1900 and severe renovations during the inter-war years. It was a rather scruffy pub lacking any personality. There were too many walls and not enough contrast; lots of floor and too little carpet. A bunch or two of flowers would have made all the difference but that could hardly have been expected from the outgoing couple. A cracked vase maybe.

But the rooms were large and airy and there was a handsome well and balcony in the big open area before the bar. A tiny snug was tucked away at the back, useful for meetings but regarded as the ladies room. The full length of the right side contained the large lounge, or concert room, as many liked to call it. The tap room at the front had a hatch servery and provided for darts, dominoes and cards. Draught beer was a penny a pint cheaper in here, or was it a penny a pint dearer in the rest of the pub? This was the scruffiest room of the lot and I was soon to learn that its neglect was due to the previous landlord's disdain (possibly dislike) of the elderly fellows who usually inhabit such bars.

'Open the front door,' said my dad.

I did it with some trepidation only to find a deserted doorstep. 'Mind the rush,' I cried, and the folks looked up. 'Only joking', I said, realising quickly that this was not a day for levity.

The Area Manager of Harrison's White Rose Brewery of Calderthorpe, which owned the Coach and Four, was Jack Thornton. He was to become a good friend and stayed around to give us what he called 'moral support'. I wondered what this meant and assumed the worst. I didn't have to wait long to find out with the arrival of our first customers. Neither Jack nor my father was to be seen and mother had long since gone to supervise domestic affairs.

There were two of them, built, as they say in the West Riding on politer days, like brick closets. Father and son at a guess and the sort of chaps to have on your side whatever was happening. 'You the new landlord?' asked the older one beaming at me.

I explained quickly enough that my father held that honour. He'd be down in a minute.

'We thought we'd introduce ourselves. The last fellow barred us for fighting but we like this pub and we've decided to come back.' It was a statement.

I understand that the blood drained from my face like the mercury in a thermometer when plunged into iced water. Hesitantly, I asked them what they wanted and served them.

'On the house are they?' said the younger one. 'Usually are when a new bloke comes in.'

Where was my father? Nobody had said anything about free drinks but they were our first customers, so throwing caution to the winds I croaked: 'Have these on me.'

'Cheers!' they responded.

'Cheers,' I squeaked.

Then my father and Jack Thornton appeared and I made perfunctory introductions.

I heard them retelling the story of being scratched by the previous landlord but I got the impression that Jack Thornton didn't believe them. And the old man, well experienced in clearing working men's clubs at closing time, didn't seem too upset either. I busied myself with some new customers but hearing laughter, looked round and saw that the four men were laughing and looking at me. I completed the round and went across to learn that I had been set up. The two men were former regulars who disliked the previous tenant and had not used the place much during his tenancy.

"The last fellow barred us but we've decided to come back"

Bob and Eric Smithies, yes they were father and son, big as they were, were as gentle as kittens. They became the most regular regulars at the Coach and Four along with their equally large wives, and were useful to have around if trouble threatened. When my parents moved on five years later, they organised a presentation and arranged a number of trips to the new pub.

Gradually the pub filled up. I got the impression that many were coming in to look at the new bosses and were short stayers. Bert Cox, the landlord of the George across the road made a brief visit, introduced himself and offered help. This time the old man bought the drinks.

Although it wasn't exceptionally busy we made the mistake of not bringing in any staff for the lunchtime session. They would have been helpful for introductions and offering warnings. But closing time came round, the doors were shut and it was time to put our feet up. I felt as if I had been on mine for a week.

Five o'clock saw the arrival of our two staff mainstays – Norman and Vera. Both had been at the Coach for some years, and both made it clear they were taking the Lowes on, rather than the Lowes employing them. 'If I don't like you,' said Vera Brockleby in her blunt West Riding manner, 'I can bugger off to some other pub tomorrow. There's plenty wanting good barmaids like me. I only stayed with the Titcheners because they paid over the odds.' No shrinking violet she.

Norman Dyson was the bar cellarman, a job he combined with self-employment in the textile business. No one quite knew what he did but whatever, it was lucrative and provided him with a modern car and a pleasant house in the better part of town – Upper Oldford. The cellar was his province and his hobby and others, even including my father, entered at their peril. He was a widower. Vera was a widow.

If we had been in a goldfish bowl at lunchtime, the evening session was to put us in the spotlight. The idea of free drinks for everyone was dismissed but, with Norman briefing us as if we were about to take the last bridge over the Rhine, it was decided to give them to most of the town's two dozen or so licensees and their spouses who were expected to visit to give us the once over. Relationships between pubs were important even though they were in competition. Mother had made large quantities of sand-wiches and snacks and these were already on the bar counters.

As most of the customers entered the pub that evening, Norman would give a run-down of their characters.

A large untidy woman came in. 'Mrs Richardson, heart of gold, drinks port and lemon, six kids and a lazy devil for a husband; he'll be in later on the scrounge.'

A small, smart man in a suit got Norman's personal attention. From the corner of his mouth came: 'Seth Sagar, Town Clerk, enjoys a couple on his way home most evenings, I'll introduce you in a minute.'

And for a healthy looking young man: 'Bernard Lynn, local cricketer, would have played for Yorkshire but sups too much for the powers that be. Nice bloke.' Thus spoke Norman the cellarer.

Bert Cox and his wife Dot were early visitors and it was good to see a relationship developing between them and my parents. They both confirmed our views on the Titcheners, whose departure that morning almost seemed an event to raise the flag for. They had their supporters, as we were to discover, but their unpopularity was, if not unanimous, certainly carried by a large majority.

Other landlords were given the Norman treatment; drinks were bought and offered in return. 'Just tell them you'll have sixpen'orth of gin,' said Norman, 'and drink soda water.' It was wise advice and the end of the evening saw me a pound better off even after paying for the drinks I'd been conned into by the Smithies earlier in the day. There were evil thoughts flashing about in my mind that this job might be more profitable than teaching. It could hardly be less.

The sandwiches vanished almost as soon as they appeared but the gesture was recognised. 'More than them other mean buggers ever did,' said one old man who took a handful without looking up from his dominoes when I took a plate of them into the tap room.

Dad and mother held court at the front of the bar, chatting to landlords, welcoming customers, listening to Norman and absorb-ing the atmosphere. I knew father was worried about folk who had been barred from this and other pubs for trouble making of vari-ous kinds who would be trying their hand at getting back into the Coach. One or two entered, saw other landlords and held back, possibly to try another day. Others came in brazenly but one stare from Norman was sufficient to send them packing. Some were shifty, allowing others to fetch drinks whilst they kept out of sight in the lounge. But we had three waiters, including Norman's nephew Brian, who were on the lookout. There was just one argument with a couple of rough-necks which the old man dealt with speedily and efficiently and started to establish for himself the reputation of a good landlord who welcomed well-behaved folk but brooked no trouble.

One crowd puzzled me. There were about a dozen of them, couples, and three or four single men. All in their twenties and early thirties, well-dressed, reasonably well-behaved and spending plenty of money.

'They're the Quality Street Gang,' said Norman. 'The local Mafia.' Nobody quite knew what they did for a living – 'in business' was the usual expression and the variety of trades in the West Riding gave plenty of scope. Most of them lived in Upper Oldford and lived rather well. I was soon to learn that they were a shady crowd and that evening we were to find out something more about the Titcheners that left them even less appealing than before.

But before that there was something else about the Coach and Four that had not been pointed out to us. It was just after ten and we were quite busy. This was not the normal Monday night scene and the following week would be a better comparison, but the staff all gritted their teeth and told us to prepare for the onslaught.

'Why?' said father.

'Because,' said Vera, 'you're the first pub in this licensing district and up t'hill in Calderthorpe they close at ten.'

The first cars were in the car park and through the door came four noisy young men demanding four pints of Best. They were followed by several more groups. None of them were drunk but all had drunk plenty before. It was unexpected and an already busy pub became a crowded one. All hands were to the pumps and by half past ten the place was humming. It set a problem, for you could hardly not serve them, but it was annoying that they should spend most of the evening and a considerable amount of money in Calderthorpe's pubs and clubs and then turn up at the Coach for last orders.

It also made the job at closing time that much more difficult.

Obviously a landlord on his first day is anxious to create a good impression with everyone, including the local police who would be keeping an eye on him. It was in the days when there was no drinking up time; the rather stupid law that allowed the purchase of alcohol up to closing time but no time after in which to drink it. Father took the diplomatic view that on such a busy night a few extra minutes wouldn't go amiss.

He reckoned without the Quality Street Gang. They took their time whilst most of the other customers went off into the night. By ten minutes to eleven they were the only ones left in the pub apart from the staff. My father approached them, asked them politely to drink up and leave. One man, slightly older than the rest, asked if he was going to lock up so that they could have another drink. Titchener always let them, two or three times a week, he claimed.

'Well,' said Alex Lowe, drawing himself up to his full five feet nine, 'I'm not Titchener and I'm not going to.'

The man, who I had decided must be the Godfather if these were the Mafia, wanted to argue, but father took no nonsense from him and politely demanded they leave. 'There's always tomorrow,' he said.

'Indeed there is,' said the man in a threatening tone. He gave the crowd a nod and they followed him to the door like sheep. There were no 'Good nights', just sullen glances.

Norman explained. Titchener had encouraged them mainly because he was not popular and couldn't attract a reasonable crowd of drinkers. He allowed them to drink after hours and there was a suspicion that one or two shady deals took place. Neither Norman nor Vera could put their finger on it but they had both seen Titchener with bottles of spirits of types not supplied by the brewery, and the purchase of these for resale was against the tenancy agreement. Norman felt it went even further and suspected that stolen goods may have changed hands.

It was an unpleasant incident and whilst we were still considering it and continuing to clear up, the local constabulary arrived. 'Just passing by, Sir,' said Sergeant Bert Powell a man we would get to like and respect.

'I'm just about to give the staff a good night drink,' said my father inviting the sergeant and his attendant constable to join us.

'Not whilst we're on duty Sir,' he replied in a tone that implied that had the constable not been with him he might have broken the code.

And so to bed, and for me the following day meant a return to Lancashire and back to school. It was fortunate that the move to the pub, which I was already beginning to feel part of, was at half term. After Easter I was moving to Leeds to teach in a high school there and could move into the pub. Until then I intended to work weekends and, if the tips continued, buy myself a little car.

Jane, the older of my sisters, kept me in touch with what happened at the pub for the rest of the week. It remained fairly busy but this was to be expected because of the novelty of a new landlord. She and the younger one, Wendy, were not to start school until the following Monday but had met their head teacher who had showed them around the school. For Jane it would be a short stay of just one term before she moved on to a secondary school. Both seemed happy enough and although they missed their friends this was partly forgotten in the hurly-burly of the move.

Weekend came quickly enough and I was back at the pub early on Friday evening. It was quite busy and I was to try my hand at waiting on. I had always admired the way in which waiters transported large tray loads of assorted drinks from bar to table and I soon discovered that this was only half of the job. The other half, of remembering the round and adding up the prices, was, for me, the difficult part. But I persevered and by the end of the evening I could cope with half a dozen drinks on a tray, even though I had to rely on the bar staff to do my adding up.

What did surprise me was the massive increase in tips to what I got when working behind the bar. 'Get yerself one mate,' was the usual invitation. A refusal brought an odd stare as if I were a brick short of a hod, and my original 'sixpen'orth of gin' appeared to give most blokes the impression that my manhood was in question. 'Get thissen a pint, lad,' I was implored and I decided that a bottle of light ale at ninepence was to become my 'tipping' drink in future.

Father had sorted out most of the undesirables with the help of Norman and Brian. The Quality Street Gang had not been back in force but one or two had been in and two couples were there that Friday. They caused no bother and left before time. But we still felt uncomfortable about them.

Saturday was reckoned to be the testing point. There were quite a lot of weekend only drinkers and it was the day that folk from further afield moved out of their own areas to drink. The full effect of being the first pub in the West Riding outside Calderthorpe had to be seen as well. Lunchtime was pleasant enough with crowds passing through on their way to the rugby league match up t'hill, and a few after shopping drinkers. Mother's sandwiches went down well and nobody seemed to mind my slipping out for a game of golf; Brian Dyson introduced me to the local club with a view to my becoming a member.

There was a gradual build-up to the evening trade. The tap room was busy and father spent some time in there with the customers. It wasn't a men only room but women were rarely seen in it. Titchener had allowed it to deteriorate in every way. The place was badly in need of decoration, the upholstery on the settles was worn and torn and needed replacing and there was a general air of scruffiness. The impression was given that it didn't need tarting up, just cleaning up. And the old lads were delighted that someone was taking an interest in them.

Several games of dominoes were being played and four younger men were at the dart board. There was a general air of contentment. No waiter was required here; they were served through the hatch and it had been the ignoring of this facility by Titchener and his wife that had been one of the biggest complaints. Most of the room's lunchtime trade had vanished and it was only in the evening, when Norman and Vera were serving, that customers appeared in the tap room.

By mid-evening on that Saturday the place was buzzing. Three waiters were serving the lounge, four of us were behind the bar and father was on sentry go throughout the pub. Norman was giving his potted biographies as new faces came in. All seemed set for a busy but pleasant evening.

We reckoned without the Quality Street Gang.

About eight of them dominated one corner of the lounge. They took up more room than they needed, but they were drinking a fair amount and there seemed no reason to do anything but leave them where they were and continue to serve them. The 'Godfather' arrived with his wife and I saw him in conversation with my father. Neither looked pleased. Afterwards it turned out that the subject of late drinking had been raised again and dad had resolutely refused any such ideas. All he got in return was an enigmatic grin.

In the course of most busy evenings a few glasses get broken, sometimes by the customers, often by the staff. It is a charge that is built into a publican's costings. That Saturday was no different to most others except that, towards closing time, two or three hit the floor in the Quality Street Gang's corner. Then a whole table went over and with it about a dozen glasses. They were full of apologies but one sensed an underlying cynicism, some of the women even giggled, despite one of them having had her dress drenched with beer. The event was left to pass. The 'gang' went home quietly enough having, as it turned out, made their point.

The last half hour rush was dealt with and after clearing up we settled down for a drink with the staff, with mother providing a stand pie and some pickles. Father tackled Norman about the Quality Street Gang. After all, he knew Oldford and he must know this mob. Was the table incident deliberate or was it a threat? Ought we to bar them? A landlord can refuse entry to whomever he pleases and he need give no reason for doing so. Norman was not his usual effusive self.

'I think you ought to talk to Bert Cox at the George about them,' said Norman. 'He had some bother with them about three years ago, then suddenly they stopped going there. I know they're a bad lot, but I can't put my finger on exactly what they're up to. Brian knew a couple of the younger blokes, having been at school with them. They always had plenty of money and were part of a group of bullies that tried to run the school,' he said. 'The younger kids had to pay threepence a week or they'd find the tyres on their bikes let down; that sort of thing.' A picture was emerging.

The following lunchtime my father and I went to see Bert Cox. We were warmly welcomed despite the impression that Bert and his wife Dot had just had a row, something we later discovered happened quite often.

'The Quality Street Gang,' said Bert, 'is a bloody nuisance. They pick on a local and put pressure on the landlord to allow them to drink late.'

'What sort of pressure?' asked father.

'It can take all forms,' said Bert, 'Annoying other customers, breaking glasses; one pub even had its large front window smashed. In my case I was foolish enough to refuse them lates while allowing a few others to have them, so they phoned the police and I was raided. I got fined with a warning from the licensing bench. I couldn't prove it was them but I'm ninety-nine per cent certain.'

The old man related last night's incident and Bert agreed that it looked as if they were trying it on. It wasn't a protection racket as such but close to it. The only way was to warn them off and father decided to bar them at the next sign of trouble.

It came that night. The gang was in early and in force and appeared initially to be behaving perfectly well. Then one of the waiters was tripped whilst passing their table. Fifteen shillings worth of drinks hit the floor to the accompaniment of laughter from the gang. Father was on hand. 'Right, you lot, Out.'

They refused and the argument raged: 'Who says?'

'I do.'

'Who are you?'

'I'm the landlord.'

'I'm a customer and I've bought drinks, I'm entitled to stay.'

'Out!'

Fortunately the Smithies, father and son, were around and with the vocal support of many other customers the old man managed to get the gang out and make it clear that they were not to return. They demanded the right to finish their drinks and were refused but given their money back. Father reckoned with the broken glasses, spilt drinks and refunds it cost him nearly a fiver but all agreed it was worth it. There was an atmosphere of relief about the place for the rest of that Sunday evening. This was how we wanted our pub to be. We had moved in.

Fifteen shillings worth of drinks hit the floor

....

THE BAR CELLARMAN'S TALE

"They also serve who only stand and wait."
JOHN MILTON'S SONNETS

NORMAN DYSON, THE PUB'S BAR CELLARMAN, knew everybody in Oldford. His nephew, Brian, who became a very good friend of mine, told me that all three of the main political parties had asked him to stand for the town council under their colours, all promising him a safe seat. He had refused them politely, implying that whilst he would continue to vote for them he preferred to keep out of active politics. Apart from membership of the Decade Club, a sort of secret drinking establishment where each member held a key to the premises, he joined nothing. 'Not even the bloody Christmas club Wilf,' he told me. But he was generous and warm-hearted and nobody in real need went short with him around.

I was introduced to his inner sanctum, as Norman liked to call the cellar, one Saturday morning while he was going through the chore of cleaning the beer lines. It was an essential but tiresome job but one which could be done much easier and quicker with two people. I became a regular. First we would empty the beer lines of their overnight water, then one of us would go upstairs to the bar and pull cleansing solution through them followed by lots of cold water. We had a system and we could move from one handpump to another without verbal contact. Then whoever was downstairs in the cellar would reconnect the pipes and we would pull through beer which needed the combined approval of the two of us before we could inflict it on the unsuspecting public.

Norman and I enjoyed our Saturday sessions and regarded the pint or so that we drank at the end as just reward for our labours. He took great pleasure on occasions in allowing customers to wait while we gave the various draught beers our nihil obstat.

'Mild OK, Wilf?' he would query.

'OK, Norman,' I would reply joining in his game.

'What about the Best?'

'Not sure about it. A bit yeasty,' was my comment showing I was picking up the jargon.

'Well we'll just pull another through then,' and so he would while the thirsty punters shuffled their feet and looked daggers at the pair of us. 'Make the buggers wait,' he would say and after pulling a pint for a bus conductor he would retort: 'He always makes me wait for his bus.' The fact that Norman had not ridden on a bus for ten years or more was not material.

"Make the buggers wait"

....

Once or twice he took me to the mysterious Decade Club. It was on the first floor of some bank chambers just off Oldford's main street. The club dated back to just after the Great War when ten friends, all former members of the Oldford 'Pals', an infantry battalion raised mainly from the businessmen of the town, had got together and decided to form a club with its own premises and to keep the membership to ten or later to units of ten. When we lived in Oldford the club had 60 members.

There was no staff except for a woman who cleaned the two Spartan rooms twice a week. No money changed hands, members served themselves, entered what they had drunk into a book and each month received a bill from the secretary. At the end of the night they would wash the glasses, empty the ashtrays and fill the shelves and there was a rota for such simple duties as admitting the draymen. The ten man committee decided on what basic policies they would follow and if some major work was needed such as redecoration then members would be levied. Guests were only allowed during the day and on special nights. Each member had a key and there were no licensing hours.

According to Norman the Decade Club was more difficult to get into than the freemasons. 'But it's a bloody sight more entertaining from what I've heard,' he said. Its members were mainly middle class, professional and businessmen, but with none of the stuffiness normally associated with such groups. I enjoyed my visits there but when I made a tentative approach about membership Norman warned me off, saying that it could be damned expensive at times, it being so easy to down a few without having to put your hand in your pocket and then, at the end of the month, along came the shock of the bill.

I went to the Christmas party. Men only of course. There was a fabulous spread and the evening was spent drinking and carousing in the pleasantest possible way. Some robust singing with a few questionable songs maybe; a genuinely funny club comedian and some good company. I spotted a notice about the evening which said that members could each bring one guest and the price, for two, would be £15. Whilst this included food, a certain amount of wine and the entertainment, it seemed an enormous amount to me but on reflection I suppose it was good value. I was only glad I didn't have a bar bill to pick up so I enjoyed myself immensely and Norman poured me home.

Brian Dyson was in many ways the opposite of Norman. Brian's parents, Norman's brother and his wife, had moved to the south of England and the young man stayed north with his uncle. Later he got his own flat but they remained good pals. But where Norman was expansive, Brian could be tight; where Norman had a few friends, Brian had many acquaintances; and whilst Norman was explosive in his humour yet discreet in his opinions, Brian would often be sarcastic and a little too outspoken. This was not to be too critical of Brian whose company I enjoyed and who fitted in well at the pub where he worked as a waiter three or four nights each week.

Brian was a wages clerk at a large carpet factory up the valley towards the Lancashire border. It was not a job he enjoyed but it demanded little of him, the hours were reasonable and the pay just about sufficient. His real ambition was to run a pub. Norman told him not to be so bloody daft but my father, who was still in the heady, early days of the job encouraged him. He thought a lot of Brian and had Norman not been there he would probably have offered him a full-time job at the pub, possibly as an assistant manager.

I eventually joined Oldford Golf Club and played with Brian most weekends and on odd evenings during the summer. He was good company if inclined on occasions to overdo things. He often drank too much and I was occasionally inclined to follow him. We got rather drunk at the golf club one Saturday afternoon when heavy rain prevented play for all but the truly adventurous. We were both due to work at the pub that evening and whilst Brian hitched a lift home to a cold shower I was foolish enough to drive the three cross country miles to the wrath of my mother.

I decided not to work and stayed upstairs with my two sisters who amused themselves at my expense. They went to bed around ten o'clock and I decided to go downstairs for a drink.

Brian was shifting loads of drinks from the bar to the lounge and looking as fit as could be. I felt like death warmed up. He smiled across at me and I nodded slowly back. Any quicker would have been disastrous.

Came closing time and when all but the staff and family were left, my mother asked me who I had been with in the golf club. I hesitated and saw Brian was hiding a smile. 'Just a few of the members,' I said. 'Nobody in particular.'

'Well, next time, do what Brian did and get yourself home in a sober condition.'

I was fit to burst but contained myself. The following morning the cheeky blighter had the nerve to ask me for a lift to the golf club to retrieve his car!

I liked Vera Brocklesby from the start. She'd had a hard life being widowed during the war with three kids to bring up. Now they had all married and flown the nest and seldom saw Vera except when they needed something. They all had kids and she loved them with a fierce intensity that was sadly not returned. Norman had more than once told Vera to 'enjoy herself'. She wasn't short of money from her cleaning jobs at two local banks and with us as a barmaid and, of course, she had a pension. It seemed that she was about to take his advice when her daughter Enid and grandson Billy landed on her doorstep after what Vera called 'the final row with that sod of a husband of hers.'

Rather than a setback the arrival of Enid and Billy seemed to make life brighter for Vera. She got on well with the pub's older patrons but the younger set thought she was a bit staid. Now she started to trade comments with them and we all noticed a new Vera. She overheard somebody say that she must have a chap hidden away at home and instead of turning nasty as she might have done before, she laughed and said that she had: 'He's three years old and looks just like his granny.'

Even so we suspected that Enid was sponging on her mother. After several weeks she was without a job and complained all the time that her husband had sent her no money. Yet she refused offers of work including one from my mother to clean the pub. Mother said she gave her the impression that it was below her dignity. 'It's not below her mother's, and she's twice the woman her daughter is,' declared a very dignified Mrs Lowe. And she was in the pub often enough spending quite freely when presumably her mother was paying.

One of Norman's other pieces of advice to Vera was to 'loosen your stays'. It meant the same thing in the metaphorical sense; to enjoy herself. But even in her present happy state she still lacked a sense of humour, often because she failed to see the joke. In our after-hours sessions the rest of us would laugh out loud and poor old Vera would sit looking querical. Norman would spell it out sometimes but still Vera just smiled indulgently.

One Saturday night we had a crowd of relatives over from South Yorkshire. They enjoyed coming to the pub and father liked having them not only for their company but because they spent well. The men were all miners and had that come-day-go-day attitude that that job engendered. After the pub closed the jokes were flying around when Vera was heard telling a story. Gradually the place went quiet. She went on: 'This chap came to the bar and asked for four pints of Best. I pulled them for him and he paid me and then got his big hands around the four glasses. I said: "Don't you want a tray?" And he said: "No thanks love, don't you think I've got enough to bloody carry?"'

The laughter started slowly and rose to a crescendo. Vera laughed loudest of all. For most of us it was the first time we had heard Vera tell a joke. For the rest of that evening she joined in the laughter and it was a good party. Just before she went home she spotted Norman. 'I meant to tell you earlier,' she said. 'But I've really enjoyed myself tonight. It must be because I've taken my corsets off.'

🐚 🐚 🐚 🐚 🐚 🐚 🐚 🐚 🐚 🐚

Mary Redmond came to work for us as a barmaid in our second week. She was mother's choice and for that matter most other folks' as well. She was pretty, intelligent, articulate and good at her job. What endeared her to most of us was her way with people.

My attempts at wooing her got a quick rebuff as a result of which we became good friends. I took great pleasure in watching the way she put down the young bloods.

'What are you doing when you finish tonight?' was one of the more polite offers she got.

'Nothing much. What did you have in mind?' she queried with a twinkle in her eye.

'How about coming out with me?' was the all too obvious response.

'Oh, no,' retorted Mary, 'I was thinking of something much more exciting like a game of chess.' And they still came back for more.

With the older blokes she had a gentler method, leaving them with the impression that they'd been propositioned. I overheard two septuagenarians discussing her. 'She really fancies me,' said one.

The other, a bit piqued at this, said: 'Well I'm not so sure about that, I think it's me she's after but in any case I'm going to bide me time.'

What we all liked about Mary was her simplicity. Despite her good looks and banter she never caused any bother, she dealt with potential trouble with an experience beyond her 25 or so years, and she kept herself to herself – few knew what she did as a day job or even where she lived.

In fact she was the youngest of a big family and the only one still living with her elderly parents in a farm cottage across the canal. She worked as the manageress of a travel agency in Calderthorpe and one of the advantages of this, she told me, was that she got plenty of free trips abroad. I asked her why she needed the evening job and she was quite open with me. 'I'm saving for the day when the old folks have gone and the farmer calls in the tied cottage so that I can buy some place of my own. And you never know,' and back came the twinkle in her eye, 'I might meet someone I fancy.'

I saw her waiting for a bus in Calderthorpe one evening and gave her a lift home. She invited me in to meet her folks and they were a delightful couple. The old man had been a farm labourer all his life and with her mother had brought up eight children. Mister Redmond kept a few hens and before I left I had a freshly baked loaf and some still-warm eggs pressed upon me – 'Our new-laid eggs were still in the hens last night,' laughed Mary's father.

I never got closer to Mary although she worked five nights a week and sometimes lunchtimes at weekends. Mother tried to persuade her to wait on tables but she stuck with bar work even though the tips weren't as good. Occasionally she would stay for lunch on Sunday when it was open house for staff. I asked her once about boy friends but got short shrift for my curiosity.

Thursday was the usual night off for Norman and Brian. One week I was talked into going for a ramble around town with them. We had called at the George and the Bluebell and we were contemplating where to go next. Everywhere Brian and I suggested met with disapproval from Norman. In the end Brian told him to decide. We went to the Dog and Duck although it was not one of our favourite haunts. Norman was in a funny mood and whilst he was in the toilet I asked Brian what was the matter? He didn't know but thought it might be something to do with work.

The evening ground to a boring close and at home I mentioned Norman's mood to the old folk. Father agreed with Brian that he might be passing through a bad phase at work, but mother thought there was something more fundamental affecting him.

'I think he's in love,' she said.

'Who with?' we asked, 'not Norman?'

'At his age?' said I, injudiciously.

'What do you mean, at his age, he's only a year older than me,' said my father. It was obviously time for bed.

Norman's wife had died in childbirth nearly 20 years before after they had been married for only two years. According to Vera it had devastated him and it took him nearly five years to show outward signs that he had got over the tragedy. Even today the inner scars remained and despite his outward displays of humour he remained basically a lonely man.

My younger sister Wendy and I had been to the library one Saturday morning when we spotted Norman in his car parked outside the office of a local building society. We were just about to cross and have a word with him when out came Mary all smiles, she got into the car and off they drove up the hill towards Norman's place. There might well have been a simple explanation for them being together I suggested to myself and Wendy, after all I had often given Mary a lift in my car. Norman often made a fuss of Wendy and she was very fond of him and now she showed a jealous streak despite being only ten years old. 'But you've not taken her to your house,' said Wendy. It was no good telling her that I had no house. I asked her to keep our little secret

That evening both Mary and Norman were on duty behind the bar. There was no obvious contact other than what might be expected amongst workmates. Mary carried on her banter with young and old alike, always giving more than she took. Norman kept the bar moving and it was a busy evening. Afterwards mother made her usual Saturday night supper but both Norman and Mary excused themselves early. Mary was tired, Norman had to drive to Manchester early on Sunday morning to see a client. They didn't leave together. No one, apart from me, appeared curious and I held my patience.

Wendy pestered me whenever we were alone. I told her to forget what we had seen but her curiosity was aroused and to tell the truth so was mine. She made a bigger fuss of Norman than usual and he responded. I told her to stop being so attentive but she claimed she didn't know what it meant! However we didn't have much longer to wait. Two weeks later I spotted Mary coming out of the County Council's Welfare Department office in the main street. 'So what?' I thought.

It was a glorious day, a Sunday morning to treasure. Before we opened the pub Norman suggested that we should close up quickly at two o'clock and all go off for lunch in the Dales. His treat, he said. 'It's not your birthday, Uncle,' said Brian, 'Why the generosity?'

'You'll see,' said Norman enigmatically.

I took my car with Mary, Vera and Brian, and Norman in his took my parents and the two girls. We headed for just outside Grassington where there was a farmhouse famed for its good English food. Norman had had the foresight to book and we were given a large table in the orchard. It was a jolly party with lots of noise. Jane had just passed her eleven-plus examination and we celebrated that. What a pity we couldn't have a drink moaned Brian and I agreed with him. 'You get too much of that anyway,' scolded my mother.

Plates loaded with ham and eggs, rump steaks and lamb chops accompanied by chips and fresh vegetables were followed by apple pies, blackcurrant pies, fresh strawberries straight from the garden and lashings of cream out of the dairy. The food was marvellous, the company was great and I agreed that we didn't need booze to enjoy ourselves like this. The girls were in ecstasy. Mary looked blooming; even Vera appeared to have loosened her stays again.

Norman vanished for a few minutes and I spotted him taking something out of the boot of his car. A few minutes later he reappeared followed by the two teenage daughters of the house. They carried trays of wine glasses and then out came the farmer and his wife, old friends of Norman. Norman produced several bottles of champagne. He looked at me. 'You wanted a drink Wilf, well here it is.' He proceeded to open the first bottle and his friend the farmer did the same with a second. No explanations arrived until all the glasses were filled. Even the girls were allowed a tiny drop.

Norman stood up and rather formally said: 'I have something very important to tell you. Mary has graciously consented to become my wife.' He was then lost for words for the first time in his life and so was Mary.

Father jumped into the breach: 'Wonderful news,' he said. 'Let me propose a toast – to Mary and Norman.' To most folk there it was entirely unexpected. Wendy and I had had our suspicions but they didn't stretch this far.

From then on the party became even rowdier and the usual questions were asked. When would the wedding be? How had they kept it quiet for so long? Who said it was so long? How long then? Long enough, said Norman.

Mary sidled up to me. 'You knew didn't you Wilf?' I told her I suspected something was on the cards but was delighted nevertheless. I warned her that Wendy might be jealous but that precocious ten-year-old seemed to be having the time of her life. Mary also told me that her parents had moved into an old peoples' home and another bit of the jigsaw fitted into place.

I could feel the eye of my mother on the back of my neck warning me not to drink too much with a car to drive. She also gave father the hard word so that he could drive Norman's car and allow the groom-to-be to enjoy himself. There was a pub to open in a couple of hours time and plenty of time later tonight for further celebrations. That evening in the pub the news brought surprise and a few broken hearts amongst young men and old. It was a very happy day.

CHAPTER 3

·······························

THE CUSTOMER'S TALE

"The customer is never wrong"
CÉSAR RITZ

ALF FOYLES WAS AN AWKWARD BEGGAR. Not in the sense that he would go out of his way to be difficult but he was contradictory. If you said there was a good chance of fine weather tomorrow, he would argue that it looked like rain; nothing more certain. Whatever the weather was tomorrow wouldn't matter because if you raised the matter with him he would prove you wrong one way or another.

Most weekday evenings he would come in around eight and order a pint of mixed. Harrisons did three regular draught beers: Bitter, Best [a light mild], and Dark Mild. And at Christmas they also produced an Old Ale of prodigious strength. Alf would drink a mix of Bitter and Dark Mild, a popular drink in the area and he was the sort of bloke that wanted everything yesterday. As he walked through the door he would expect you to start pulling his pint regardless of the needs of other customers.

He wasn't vindictive but he would enjoy taking you down a peg or putting one over on you. One Friday I was alone in the bar when Alf came in. I started to pull the bitter into a pint glass. Strictly speaking we ought to have pulled two halves and then mixed them in a pint glass, but no one had ever complained and Alf certainly would have done at the extra time such a process would have taken.

I moved to add the mild when Alf said: 'I'll have a pint of Best.'

No 'please' or 'sorry'.

'But...' I stuttered.

'Never mind buts,' he said, 'A pint of Best.'

He paid for it with the exact money which I suspect he had in his hand before he entered the pub and with a sardonic smile he sat down. As was his usual practice he left after one drink to move to other pubs further into town. My reputation in falling for the set-up was growing.

Alf believed he was a bit of a practical joker though it was not an opinion shared by many others, mainly because he was something of a loner. He was seldom in company and always only bought his own beer and refused it from other folk. Even at Christmas when Dad bought all his regulars a drink he would offer a tentative refusal before accepting. One Saturday morning however he surprised me.

The old man had been under pressure to install a jukebox. The brewery managers wanted him to as they took a cut of the profits and there would also be something in it for him. He was conservative in his attitude and, I suspect had what he believed was the interests of his customers in mind. Eventually he agreed to have one in for a two-month trial with speakers in the lounge and main bar but not in the tap room or snug. The record selection was what the disc jockeys would call 'middle of the road.'

Alf Foyles wasn't a regular on Saturday lunchtimes but he came in that day in a more affable mood than usual. There were no attempts to catch me out with his choice of drink and he wore a cheeky grin that was right out of character. The bar was very quiet.

'Wilf,' he said, calling me by name for the first time ever, 'this new juke box – who picks the records?'

I explained that there were lists offered of various kinds of music and the landlord chose from them including, if he liked, some of his own.

'So, if you wanted to put a particular record in the box, you could do so?'

I wondered what he was getting at and as I pondered he went on: 'What if you wanted to change one of those that are in there now. Could you open the box and swop one?'

I wasn't sure but told him that I imagined you could. It turned out that father had a key to gain access to the works but not to the money. This was kept by the leasing company who wanted their cut. I eventually lost my patience and came out with: 'Stop beating about the bush Alf, and tell me what you're on about.'

His idea was this. He had a record of the Sistine Chapel choir singing the Gloria and the Agnus Dei from some obscure mass. How about swopping it for some popular record, such as one of Frank Sinatra's, and seeing what the lads made of that. Could we do it without anyone else finding out? Was I prepared to have a go?

The idea appealed to me but it had to be kept secret from my parents although I realised that inevitably they would find out. The key was on father's large bunch but as he often gave them to me for opening or locking up the pub it would be an easy matter to remove it and it was unlikely that it would be missed. OK, I agreed, but when? We decided on the following lunchtime – a Sunday – when the pub was reasonably busy with the swop being made during the morning. I would arrange to borrow the key that afternoon when I closed up the pub.

Record 54 showed that it had two Sinatra hits on it. It got a reasonable amount of plays with one song being top of the hit parade but now its actual music was known only to Alf Foyles and me. There was every chance that Sinatra would be selected at least once in that session. In fact we didn't have to wait long. One of a gang of four young sparks started playing the box and the second choice was our joker. The prosaic music crackled out. Heavens, I thought, he must have had this record since 45s were first invented.

'Who put this on?' bawled Alf and the lads all pointed at the innocent culprit. The pub went quiet and then laughter gradually broke out.

'I could have sworn I put on Frank Sinatra,' said the hapless lad.

'Well make sure you do next time,' said Alf. It seemed we were going to have a repeat.

'Right, here goes,' said the dupe, 'Number fifty-four, Francis Albert Sinatra singing 'Three Coins in the Fountain.' And on again came the scratchings of the Sistine Chapel choir. Alf Foyles was beside himself and as I seemed to be in charge that lunchtime I decided to let it run. As it happened nobody else wanted to hear Sinatra that session and the lads spent an unprofitable half hour trying to find which record they had been conned into paying for.

Later on that afternoon I swapped the records back and returned the jukebox key to father's key ring. The next time Alf encountered the four lads in the pub he took great pleasure in selecting the Sinatra record and asking in a loud voice: 'What happened to that church music we used to have on in here?'

On Sunday lunchtimes it was a standard practice in the pubs of the area to provide free food for the customers. Nothing too elaborate; two or three loaves of bread and a couple of pounds of cheese and some pickled onions or maybe a piece of brisket straight from the oven. Customers would cut their own and most were practised in the art of knowing exactly how much to take. Come late and all was gone.

Mother used to alternate between cheese and meat and around Christmas she would provide a couple of stand pies and maybe a stuffed pig's head which was a popular local dish. On hot summer Sundays an alternative might be slices of cold black pudding, lumps of cheese, spring onions and radishes. There was always plenty of salt just to show that publicans weren't entirely altruistic. Father reckoned the food more than paid for itself in addition to being a good public relations exercise.

The various pubs vied with one another to provide either better food or something unusual. One Sunday Dot Cox had French mustard to accompany her piece of beef; the following week my mother had freshly grated horseradish. At the Dolphin there was farmhouse Wensleydale (or so they said) so the Bluebell followed up with Stilton. Red cabbage accompanied the food at the Dog and Duck and home-pickled onions that at the Throstle's Nest. Ma Gamp – I never did find out her real name – at the Rising Sun, went to Burgundy on a Licensed Victuallers Association trip and a week later Quiche Lorraine adorned her bar. 'Tasted like sour custard,' said one of our regulars making a face. He had been sent out to spy by my mother.

The first customer one Sunday at the Coach and Four was a stranger, not too well dressed and looking as if he could use a square meal. He ordered a half of Best and was invited by the barman to help himself to the brisket of beef. He cut a thick slice off it to make himself a substantial sandwich and remained at his commanding position in front of the joint. Two or three regulars hovered but politely waited. The stranger finished his sandwich and proceeded to carve himself another thick slice. He noticed the hungry looks of his companions, grinned at them, 'This is good,' he said, 'when are they fetching thine?'

One could never be sure if the man concerned was having us on or whether he was genuine that he thought that the piece of beef was solely for him. The bloke who annoyed my father the following Christmas Eve was certainly in no doubt.

The pig's head was big and delicious. Freshly baked bread and what mother called 'best butter' was there in plenty and there were accompaniments of chutney, apple sauce, stuffing and mustard. The man was an occasional customer, certainly not a regular. He lived locally and was known to work his way around the pubs on Sundays sampling the free food and saving himself the bother and cost of providing his own lunch. On this seasonable occasion it seemed he was stocking up for the next few days as well.

My father watched the man make a large sandwich with all the trimmings to accompany his half pint of beer. After a short interval he came back for another equally as large. He was not the only one to visit the groaning board twice but the others were regulars and had been encouraged to do so by my father.

The old man must have anticipated what was going to happen next for he took over the job of preparing the sandwiches. He was a bit noisy about it: 'Let me help you to another Jack,' he would say. Or: 'Here, Fred, have one of these – a bit more stuffing on it?' And the like. He kept one eye on your man.

Eventually, as father had foreseen, the man came up for a third sandwich. The landlord was sweetness and light. 'Another sandwich, sir? A spot of stuffing? Mustard? Just a little. Here we are, enjoy it sir,' he prattled on, passing over the sandwich.

What nobody but father knew was that the bottom slice of bread had been lavishly 'buttered' with mustard. But the customer was soon to find out with his first bite. He gasped and screamed an expletive. Father played the innocent and handed over a pint of bitter saying: 'Too much mustard sir? Well drink that down you. That's just one and a penny please.'

The man, still gasping, took one look at my father, scowled and left the pub. 'Bar him in future' was my father's immediate instruction to the staff. 'Anyone for another sandwich?' was his invitation to the rest of the Christmas Eve customers. It was a little while before there were any takers.

Mother was anxious to use the pub to its full by catering for what she called 'special occasions'. She let it be known that the Concert Room was available for weddings, birthday parties, christenings, even funerals. If necessary she would provide the food in which case the room was free. If the party preferred to do their own catering then she charged for the room. The main source of profit came from over the bar particularly since the old man could usually obtain an extension of his licence to serve during the afternoon.

Most weddings in the West Riding seemed to be held on a Saturday, particularly just before the end of the tax year. The Parish Church, the Catholic Church, the Methodist Chapel and

"Too much mustard sir?"

the tiny Unitarian Chapel as well as the Register Office were all busy on spring and summer Saturdays and the adjacent pubs as well. We were fortunate as the Parish Church was next-door-but-one and next to that was the registry office. We even picked up a fair amount of trade from folk awaiting weddings at these two venues that had receptions elsewhere. All this made for brisk business for the Coach and Four.

But these 'special occasions' were a mixed blessing. Most of them were for regulars at the pub whom we knew and usually trusted. But we were often approached by others who preferred the pub's facilities to those of a church hall or community centre. Whilst it was possible to check on the folk who used the pub in the ordinary course of events and to refuse service to those who failed to meet the landlord's standards – and the list of those the old man barred was fairly short – it was impossible to judge a wedding party of strangers until it was in full swing.

We had one where the rather pretty, shy bride-to-be came to see my mother and booked a quite lavish spread for 60. It was a sit-down do with sherry on arrival and champagne for the toast. She took on extra staff and father looked forward to a good return over the bar.

Came the day and around half past two the first guests started drifting in looking as if they had been at the booze for some time already. They had. They also looked as if they were from a couple of rough families who lived on the top estate who had been daggers drawn for years. They were. It didn't take long for us to suspect that there might be some trouble. There was.

Attempts by the two families to keep the bride and groom apart had failed and looking at the inevitable it had been agreed that the wedding should go ahead. It was held at noon in the local Catholic Church but most of the young bloods, and some older ones too, had stoked up from opening time in the Rising Sun where Ma Gamp was not too particular about her customers.

In fact, what had happened on this occasion was that we had been set up. The two families in making their arrangements for the wedding knew that it would be difficult to book a pub for the reception. So the young bride had been sent to book the room, arrange the menu and the drinks and even make a show of good faith by paying a substantial deposit. It turned out that the address she gave was that of a most respectable teetotal spinster who happened to have the same surname as herself and whose name she had taken from the phone book. The families had gone to some trouble.

All went well for the first hour or so, with the sherry being downed quickly enough and the drinkers moving into the bar during the hiatus before lunch. A few of the regulars displayed their disquiet but father ushered them into the tap room and the snug. Mother pushed forward with the meal and we got them sat down. Food seems to have a soporific effect on even the rowdiest of folk and so it was with this party. It was only when the speeches began that the trouble started.

The bride's family were very proud of her, deservedly so for she was extremely pretty and seemed a bright lass with a perky nature. The best man, who was the groom's elder brother, had been one of the main opponents of the wedding. 'He fancied her himself,' said another guest later in the day. The best man's first job after the meal was to read out the telegrams and messages of good wishes. The first one was a spoof probably inserted by himself. He read: 'Good wishes Larry on your wedding – what a pity you had to choose such an ugly cow.'

He didn't manage to read on to say who had sent it because of the row that broke out from the bride's relatives. The brother had enough sense for the moment to shout out above the noise that he thought it must have been a joke. He then carried on with the rest of the genuine messages but couldn't resist dropping a sarcastic remark towards the end about what he regarded his brother's chances would be that night in bed. That was the final spark so far as the bride's family were concerned. A glass was thrown at the best man which fortunately only struck him on the shoulder but it was the sign for a full-scale battle to break out.

Tables were uptipped; plates were smashed over heads; punches were thrown, caught and returned; mayhem reigned. Everyone joined in; men, women and children. As an onlooker I had no idea who was fighting who but it was certain that the participants did. One of our barmen who attempted to separate a pair of young men found himself turned on at by both of them. He got out of the way quickly to see them fighting one another again.

Father's immediate reaction was to phone the police but he had an intelligent instinct that warned him that if he came right out with who was fighting the boys in blue might not be too enthusiastic in responding. Fights between these families were legion and better sorted out between themselves. So he merely said there was trouble at the pub and could they help out.

In the event two uniformed lads came along pretty quickly and an immediate request from them brought four more. With the help of some of the larger customers, including the ever-helpful Bob and Eric Smithies, some sort of order was restored.

The wedding party – or parties as they now were – were asked to leave. One middle-aged woman who turned out to be an aunt of the bride had the audacity to ask for the champagne. Mother pointed out in strident tones that only a deposit had been paid and there was still quite a bit owing for the meal, and there was a considerable amount of damage to the pub to be paid for as well. A general view was that the prospect of either being paid was unlikely and that we were lucky that the champagne hadn't been opened.

The police decided to prosecute seven men and two women. The men included the best man and the groom's father and one of the women was the bride's mother. The only person present who had no connection with either side was the priest who had performed the wedding ceremony and the joke went round that he was very lucky to have escaped prosecution as well.

Both my parents, a waitress and a customer gave evidence; all nine were found guilty and received hefty fines and ordered to pay a substantial sum towards the damages. My father still awaits the damages. My mother still awaits the balance of the bill for the wedding breakfast. The happy couple moved into a house across the valley as far away from their families as possible and as far as we know live happily ever after.

🍺🍺🍺🍺🍺🍺🍺🍺🍺🍺

Funerals were a different matter. My mother told me that she could not remember one of the dozen or so she catered for during the five years they were at the Coach and Four that did not finish up as a happy occasion. They usually started with quite a bit of weeping and sadness, but the alcohol loosened tongues and memories of happier times past were related.

Such was the case of Ben Findon, a happy soul who graced the pub most days of his life and who lived to his late seventies before succumbing to a stroke one afternoon on the bowling green. His widow, Doris, came round with her eldest son to say that Ben would have wanted his funeral tea to be at the Coach because of the many happy hours he spent there.

It would have been easy to fall into a slough of sentimentality when discussing such matters. The customers, on the one side, are mourning a not yet buried and closely-attached soul and are fallible, whereas the licensee in feeling sorry for them could easily be moved into saying: 'They've got enough troubles, I can do this at very little profit and help them out.' Another view is that the licensee has the mourners at his mercy, they are at a low point, and can happily overcharge. A sense of balance is required.

My mother discussed the arrangements with the Findons and they agreed a reasonable price for a buffet tea to follow the cremation at Calderthorpe. It was to be in the afternoon but father took the view that an extension of licence was not necessary – if drinks were required then he was prepared to serve them. About 30 people were expected to come back.

It was a pleasant enough afternoon and the pub had only just closed when the funeral party arrived. Norman and I had been to represent the staff and family of the Coach and Four. Mrs Findon was visibly upset and was being comforted by her sister and a daughter-in-law. The men were more stoic and father was soon into business at the bar.

Inevitably the old tales started to circulate. 'I remember Ben as a lad,' said one old chap.

'Well thar'll be next then,' said his slightly younger mate. The conversation moved to the contemporary scene.

One colleague related some of Ben Findon's exploits on the bowling green: 'He played every day it were fit to play,' he said, 'And he always turned out for t'team when asked.'

'He were playing for t'team on t'day he died,' said another friend, and a sudden hush amongst the men at the bar made most folk realise that memories of that particular day were probably best left untold for the moment. But the sense of propriety had not reached the speaker. 'In fact,' he went on, 'He were 19 to 12 in front and had he finished his game we'd have won t'bloody match.'

🍺 🍺 🍺 🍺 🍺 🍺 🍺 🍺 🍺 🍺

Occasionally my mother would have two or three lodgers at the pub. She didn't particularly like the idea what with two young girls around the place but, if she knew them and felt she could trust them, then some rooms on the top floor were made available.

Tommy and Hughie were a pair of likeable Ulstermen. In a sense they were already tenants of ours because they rented two of the garages at the back of the car park and the loft above them. They drank a lot in the pub, but never seemed to get drunk, held no strong political views and were happy to live in the West Riding. They had a darker side that we never looked into although I wondered at times if my father ought to be more circumspect. They worked the markets in the West Riding and over into Lancashire with regular pitches – Ashton on Monday, Dewsbury on Tuesday, and so on – selling tinned goods such as fruits, vegetables, fish and meat.

Their rent of two pounds a week for the garages was seldom paid in cash. Often a large box of tinned fruit or something similar would be offered and usually gratefully accepted. With a growing family and relatives often over for the weekends such food was needed. My mother's large larder was always full: baked beans, Italian tomatoes, peach halves, corned beef, sardines, you name it.

I was talking to the pair of them one evening when Hughie told me how they had just done a deal with a man from Barnsley who had offered them about ten thousand tins with assorted contents for an amazingly cheap price. The trouble was it was stock rescued from a flooded warehouse and hardly any of the tins had labels on them. They had opened and tested several tins and they were all in good order.

Many of the tins such as those containing corned beef and sardines were easy to identify and most of the very large ones contained fruit. But this left a problem, as just about half of the goods could be anything although they had been given a categorical assurance that there was no pet food included. They came up with an idea but had to be a bit careful where they tried it out. Twenty tins of assorted sizes would go into a box and would be sold for one pound as a 'mystery food hamper'. 'You pays your money and you takes your pot luck', joked Tommy with a loud laugh.

There were two markets where they could sell their hampers at which the inspectors weren't too inquisitive for despite the average layman's lack of knowledge of the law, they were sure that what they were doing was 'not quite on the line,' as Hughie put it. Tommy nipped out and fetched a box that he gave to my mother, who promptly took it upstairs. She too had her doubts and warned the lads not to try selling any in the pub as they often did with the legitimate items.

I had my doubts too, not just about the business of selling 'mystery' goods but where they actually came from in the first place. The Irishmen weren't dishonest in the sense that they would rob someone or even try to work a fiddle, but they didn't bother too much about the niceties of commerce.

I discussed it with my parents because I was worried about the 'mystery food hampers' being stored on what were technically the brewery's premises. Father's easy going nature shone through and he decided to leave things be because at the rate they were moving the 500 or so boxes would be gone in a couple of weeks. Fortunately he was right, although for the next two or three weeks when the lads tried to pay the rent with a couple of 'hampers' the old man resisted.

Our hamper remained untouched for months. Occasionally the girls and I would try and persuade mother to open one of the tins but she resolutely refused and at Christmas she handed over the full box to the folk at the Methodist Church who organised an appeal for the old folk of the town. On Christmas Day father carved the turkey and we enjoyed a bottle of Irish whiskey that the lads had paid their rent with before sailing off to Belfast for the festivities. I kept back a wry smile at the thought of some dear old soul opening what she thought to be a tin of peach halves for the Christmas tea only to find it contained chopped tomatoes.

The snug at the back of the long bar which held about 20 people was always known as the 'Ladies Room'. It wasn't exclusively for women and the darts and domino players used it for their meetings; it was available for small private parties and it was also a useful place to lay out buffet meals. But on most weekday evenings it was used by a coterie of elderly women who treated it as a sort of distaff tap room but grumbled because, unlike the men, they got no reduction in the price of drinks. My mother put in a television set to stop their moans.

One Sunday night a party of women from a pub in Burnley called in on their return from a trip to Scarborough. Mother opened up the snug and drafted me in to wait on them. They were a lively lot and sat around in fours and fives drinking halves of Best, light ales and assorted shorts.

The visiting landlady who had had a few already was in the main bar chatting with a couple of her cronies and my mother. She was in an expansive mood, loquacious and noisy. I was beckoned by her and told to tell the ladies in the snug that their landlady was buying a round. Suddenly the order changed to pints and doubles! Feeling a bit peeved at having to work I added one for myself on the grounds that this was supposed to be my night off. The round came to four pounds seventeen shillings and when I told the landlady she gave me five pounds and told me to keep the change. I felt a bit of a heel.

🍺🍺🍺🍺🍺🍺🍺🍺🍺🍺

Gertie spent many hours in the snug but didn't drink a lot. What she did buy she made last. To hear her talk you would think that she was being gracious in allowing us her custom. She must have been in her late seventies and claimed to have been a star of the music hall in what she called 'the old days'.

'They must have been very old days,' said Norman Dyson, 'because nobody in this town remembers her.' But she had that lower middle class accent that one associates with stage folk even though she wore lower working class clothes.

Her drink was 'a small port with hot water, dear,' and she made it last all night. Often she would be the only one in the snug watching the television and complaining about the cold. She lived in a council flat across the canal and mother reckoned she saved a fortune on heating bills by spending most Autumn, Winter and early Spring evenings in the Coach and Four. 'And we make nothing out of her with her one measly drink each night,' she complained.

She was heartily disliked by the other women in the snug, mainly because she tried to lord it over them. Despite all this I liked Gertie and occasionally tried to get her to talk about her days on the stage. She was losing a bit of memory but it was obvious she had spent some time in the footlights if only as a chorus girl. I offered to buy her a drink and she took me for a brandy as if she were doing me a favour and regaled me with romances of how in her day she had drunk magnums of champagne bought by her many admirers.

On cold days she often came in at lunchtimes and sat in the snug without attempting to catch attention. The drink wasn't important but the welcoming gas fire was. If she were spotted she was asked what she was having and she felt obliged to buy her usual, otherwise she would simply sit there without a drink. One winter's day she settled herself without anybody noticing. It was quiet and at closing time father locked up and went upstairs for his lunch and a snooze. Mother was in Calderthorpe for the day.

It was well after seven o'clock before anyone spotted Gertie. She had made herself very comfortable, taken off her shoes, folded up her coat as a pillow and was happily snoring away on one of the settles alongside the fire. She offered an apology saying she must have nodded off but there was a suspicion that she had done it deliberately and secretively. After that we were more careful when locking up the pub and kept an eye on Gertie.

Every year while we were at the Coach and Four there was a trip to the Rugby League cup final at Wembley. It didn't really matter who was playing; what was important was that there were good tickets and a decent hotel in London. The trip left on Friday lunchtime and was home by teatime on Sunday. The week after the match arrangements started for the following year's trip.

Suddenly the order changed to pints and doubles!

The organiser was Denis Roberts who in his younger days after playing for Wales at rugby union, had signed for one of the top league sides and had a successful career in the game. Now he kept a newsagent's in Oldford's main street and enjoyed a pint or two in the Coach. He lived with his wife Lois and their two kids and Lois's father Billy Rees. Billy, better known as 'Digger', was a retired miner who had lost a leg in a pit accident many years before and who had continued to dine out, or rather drink out on the story ever since.

....

Places on the trip were not easy to come by. It was very popular and vacancies were soon filled. Each participant paid in whatever amount they wanted each week provided it was enough to cover the cost of transport, tickets and hotel. The balance, as Digger Rees said, 'was for boozing.' Denis collected the money but the landlord was the treasurer, a practice that came about after a previous trip organiser did a bunk two weeks before the event but not far enough away to escape the long arm of the law.

It was mainly for men but a small number of women came along. The chauvinists said they were the wives of blokes who wouldn't otherwise be allowed to go. Whatever the reasons they added a bit of colour to the proceedings and kept the behavioural standards higher than they would otherwise have been. One fellow got ribbed for weeks when his wife went to the match in her curlers maintaining that she wanted to look her best for the evening session in the hotel.

I was too late to go on the first trip that took place shortly after we moved into the pub but both my father and I were accepted for the next one. We went on all the others while we were at the pub and they were very enjoyable occasions. We left a young man behind once after he 'fell in love' with a barmaid at the hotel and another time a young couple missed the match at Wembley because they claimed they had got lost in London on Saturday morning. As they were recently married there was a suspicion that they never left the hotel. But, on the whole, the trips were smoothly organised and little went wrong.

When the local side in nearby Calderthorpe made it to the final we were all glad we had booked our places months before. Not only were tickets in short supply but it was almost impossible to book a coach and reasonably priced accommodation in London was scarce. The town was alive and everyone was looking forward to a great weekend. All that we needed was a win.

Sadly that was not to be but it was a great game and the Calderthorpe team was not disgraced by the scoreline of 20 points to 16. We were in a buoyant if not ecstatic mood on returning to the hotel for dinner and what we had hoped would be the night's celebrations. But most of us were prepared to make the best of it and the younger crowd took off to a pub in Camden Town where there was a cabaret.

Sunday brought rain, some sore heads and a few glum faces. The coach left at ten aimed for Grantham where lunch had been booked in a large pub. The result of the final was sinking in and there was a move to skip lunch and head straight back home but this was soon quashed by Denis Roberts and a few of us who not only wanted value for our money but were happy to keep the drinking going for as long as possible.

*Went to the match in her curlers
to look her best for the evening*

The long faces were there at lunch and calls of 'hurry up, let's get back on the bus,' were, I'm glad to say, largely ignored. Digger Rees knew a working men's club that remained open until three and welcomed parties. The moon faces objected and a compromise was reached that we would leave at two. Norman and Brian Dyson and I and around a dozen others followed Digger down to the club. The comedian was a bit blue but when he knew that our crowd were in he then made us the butt of his jokes by dwelling on Calderthorpe's defeat. But we enjoyed ourselves.

Came a quarter to two and some of the crowd started to move off. Digger Rees finished his drink and made to get up. 'Where's my crutch?' he cried. 'Come on now, don't play silly beggars, who's got my crutch?' We looked all around but the single crutch that Digger used had vanished.

'Better have another then until we find it,' suggested his son in law, Denis Roberts, and so we did.

Two o'clock passed and another round was ordered and the reason for the delay seemed to have been overlooked. Then in came one of the long faces demanding to know why the devil we weren't back at the bus.

'Digger's lost his crutch,' slurred Brian Dyson.

'And I suppose you lot are looking for it,' exploded the long face.

'Well we were,' said Brian, 'but we can't find it. Whose round is it?' The long face stamped out.

Just before three Denis Roberts went to attend to a call of nature and returned with Digger's crutch. 'It warinth'bogs,' he mumbled, 'Berrerhavernother.' So we did and then made our erratic way back to the bus and a somewhat chilly reception. And our crowd didn't endear itself to the others by the constant calls for comfort stops on the rest of the journey.

Back in Oldford I reflected on what a good weekend it had been and the thought that some of the long faces were going to have to explain their late arrival home although it was no fault of their own – but serve them right I thought.

The following night Calderthorpe Council held a civic reception for the team and the players paraded through the town in an open-topped bus. One of the long faces decided to go and watch and Digger Rees asked him for a lift.

'Not on your life,' he replied, 'Why don't you walk, then you'll be certain not to lose your crutch.'

Fat Eddie had problems getting a drink in Oldford although it really wasn't his fault. It was all the fault of Little Minnie. They were an unlikely coupling. Eddie was well over six feet tall and weighed around seventeen stone, Minnie was as thin as a wisp and barely topped five feet. He was placid. She was explosive.

They were in their thirties and had lived together for ten years or so. Eddie was a casual labourer working on road construction and he earned good money when he chose to. Minnie went out of her way to help him spend it. Eddie on his own was no problem. He would wander around town and have a pint or two in the pubs that he was currently allowed in, chatting about any number of topics and being thoroughly agreeable. Most landlords in Oldford barred Eddie and Minnie but Eddie on his own was usually permitted.

Minnie was the bother. Two drinks and she would start an argument with anyone but usually with one of the bar staff, more particularly with the licensee. It was never a malicious argument; it was often something quite trivial, but when she started she really let rip.

I caught the back end of one row when my father – 'I'll never let her in again' – had succumbed to the silver-tongued persuasiveness of Fat Eddie.

Minnie was screaming that there was no gin in her gin and tonic. 'It's just tonic,' she bellowed at my father, 'You've twisted me.'

The calm and logical suggestion that she was pretty well gone considering she had only been drinking tonic water brought further fury. Minnie was told to leave and once more she was barred for an indefinite period.

Eddie's pleas on Minnie's behalf were always laced with 'She's very sorry,' and 'She'll never do it again.' But most landlords found to their cost that she couldn't help herself. Many folk contemplated on why Eddie stayed with her but it was obvious, to me at least, that he was genuinely fond of her, very protective and no doubt saw some of his affection returned in their privacy. When Minnie blew up he would never try to interfere and calm her down, for he would then become the butt of her temper which would be redoubled.

The police knew all about Minnie but they had never arrested or charged her, mainly because she was never violent, just loud, abusive and argumentative. They had to put her straight occasionally and show her the doors of several pubs, but she had a clean record and, for that matter, so did Eddie.

They lived in a small cottage on the south side of the canal and no one else to my knowledge had ever been in it. The couple had no real friends and Eddie's only acquaintances were the men he worked with. If they had relations they were a long way away.

For several weeks Fat Eddie was seen around town, usually on his own except on Fridays at early doors when the road gang would have a few to celebrate pay day. Little Minnie was not around and not much missed.

I bumped into Eddie in the Big Crown and struck up a conversation with him about rugby league. I was not surprised to discover that he had played a bit when he was younger as a prop forward and had trials for a professional club. 'But I was a bit too slow for them,' he drawled.

I offered a cautious question. 'How's Minnie?'

'Fine,' he said, 'in the pink. It won't be long now.'

I was curious. 'What won't be long?'

'The baby, of course;' responding as if all the world knew about it. Minnie's absence from the pub and argument scene was explained. It turned out that a baby was expected in a couple of weeks and that Minnie looked in Eddie's words: 'Like an upside down question mark with legs.'

The consequences were, I suppose, inevitable. When the chubby little lad was born he came into a world of calmness and love. His father occasionally went for a drink with his workmates but his mother was sworn off the booze for ever. She was doting, caring and full of affection and no child wanted for a better home.

Given the chance on summer weekdays my father would be off to Headingley or Park Avenue in Bradford to see Yorkshire play cricket. In the nineteen thirties he had played league cricket in both the West Riding where he was born and later in Lancashire where he moved to. He had trials for Yorkshire and played half a dozen games for the second eleven. But you had to be very good to make it good with Yorkshire in those days.

He was very proud of his cricketing ability but was honest enough to say that a century in the Yorkshire Council gave him a good deal more satisfaction than twenties and thirties for Yorkshire seconds. But though his playing days were over, his love for the game was as intense as ever. He joined the Oldford Cricket Club, watched them when he could and did a bit of coaching with the younger players.

Bernard Lynn was the captain of Oldford CC, a middle of the road club in the Central Yorkshire League, and he was a regular at the Coach and Four. Norman Dyson often said that Bernard would have been a county player but his face didn't fit with the 'powers that be' because he liked his ale too much.

It was, according to Bernard, a trait that kept many good players out of the team although he admitted that a place on the Yorkshire staff was a difficult thing to achieve whatever one's personal tastes and predilections. Like my father some years earlier he had made the trek to the county nets at Headingley, been coached by Maurice Leyland and Arthur Mitchell but after a handful of second team appearances he had been told: 'Don't ring us, we'll ring you.' Whether it was his habit of having the odd pint or two after training and matches or whether he just wasn't good enough had ceased to worry him.

Bernard Lynn was a worrying, persistent and very accurate slow left arm bowler and a forceful middle order batsman. He captained the side with authority and demanded respect on the field but afterwards he was the life and soul of the party and all men were equal. The club had just had a good season, finishing third in the league and runner up in the knock-out cup, but the juniors had won their league and things for the club looked promising.

My father suggested a celebratory supper at the Coach for the players. So long as everyone was 14 years of age or over and the room was kept private there would be no problem with the law and the younger players would be sent home at a reasonable hour to enable the rest to carry on enjoying themselves. It seemed a great idea.

Bernard welcomed it and members of the club were delighted. Facilities at the cricket club were quite limited; there was no bar and catering finished at the tea and sandwich level and over recent years the players had tended to gravitate to the Coach, regarding it as 'their pub'. My mother decided on a simple hot pot with pickles and red cabbage followed by apple pie and Wensleydale cheese. The brewery, in the shape of Jack Thornton its area manager, agreed to buy a round of drinks, the cricket club did the same and so did a couple of other landlords. It had the makings of a great evening.

My declared intention of being there was met with disapproval from my father. 'On what grounds?' he asked. 'You're not a member of the cricket club. Why should you be there any more than say, Len Hutton, whom I'm sure the players would be delighted to have as their guest.' I felt somewhat put down but recovered fast and said I was prepared to work that evening. 'I already had you down for the washing up,' retorted father.

Came the evening and the room was decked out with cricket memorabilia, photographs of teams long gone, posters advertising ancient games, trophies from the club's former triumphs and, in pride of place, the junior section cup. The club had decided to award commemorative medals to the junior team and had asked my father to present them.

The supper was a great success. The juniors were delighted with their medals; they enjoyed the company of the senior players and felt very grown up for the evening. The junior captain who many felt had great potential and had already had some good scores with the senior sides, made a confident speech of thanks and even joked that come next season members of the first eleven would have to look to their metal.

After the juniors departed the drinking and carousing began in earnest. Bernard Lynn proposed a toast to all Yorkshiremen in the side, which drew a response from the vice captain who was a Londoner to 'not forget the help the club got from foreigners like himself'. This drew derisory whistles and jeers until he pointed out that he and the only overseas player – a forcing West Indian bats-man – had made the highest partnership of the season, and a club record to boot.

It was that sort of evening. Good conversation, plenty of banter, lots of drink and if a little boisterous then this was accept-able. It finished with a cricket match down the centre of the concert room when the tables were cleared. It was probably the shortest match ever played.

Someone produced a boy's bat and a ball was manufactured from paper napkins wrapped with sticky tape. A chair acted as the wicket. My father opened the batting to the bowling of Bernard Lynn. The first ball was driven straight back over Bernard's head. He jumped up to catch it and caught a light bulb instead. The language was not for children's ears. My father declared his innings at four runs for no wickets, Bernard Lynn retired hurt and my mother suggested, nay demanded, in as many words, that the match be declared a draw.

TAP ROOM TALES

"…the mysterious local world of the vault,
the tap room or the public bar. "
PUB GAMES – ARTHUR TAYLOR

HARRY SMITH HAD TWO OR THREE pints in the tap room every lunchtime, Sunday to Saturday, summer and winter, rain, hail or shine. From the day my father moved into the pub Harry had never missed a day. He was long retired and lived with his long-suffering wife in a cottage just behind the Coach and Four. The only time you saw him in the pub in an evening was when he was persuaded by his wife to take her for a port and lemon. Harry didn't really hold with women in pubs.

One May morning he confided in father that, much against his better judgement, he and the missus were going to Scarborough for a week. 'Can't think why she wants to go there,' he moaned, 'Or anywhere else for that matter. It's too early for cricket and too late for football. Pubs in Scarborough are no great shakes and I'm bloody certain landlords water their beer for t'holiday season.' Harry was not a happy man.

However the fateful day arrived and, with the cardboard suit-case tied up with string, off the couple went on the bus to Scarborough to sample the delights of the Chestnut Tree Guest House. Several folk remarked that the tap room seemed empty without Harry.

Came Monday lunchtime and he was back. Father quizzed him: 'What the devil are you doing here, I thought you'd gone for a week?'

'We have,' said Harry. 'But this morning we got on one of them there mystery trips. When we got to Malton, driver said we were off to Hardcastle Crags stopping for lunch in Oldford. So the missus has gone home to make a pot of tea and some sandwiches and I've come in here for a pint.'

Charlie Worth was a careful man, in so far as it concerned his drinking. And he was the archetypal Yorkshireman. He drank alone, though not too many, and only when he could afford it. What is more he had a wife and nine kids to support, so it was said that occasionally he had not been too careful.

He was at home in the tap room where he could hold his own in the conversation and arguments. Charlie worked on the railway, in the absolute sense, for he was a platelayer. He took every opportunity to pick up overtime for he put family first and self second. And to eke out the income he had a secondary occupation which he didn't shout about for certain legal reasons and because of the feeling often held in small towns that such activities could win you a few friends but plenty of enemies, particularly amongst established and full-time tradesmen. Charlie repaired boots and shoes.

He only did it for a few folk, mostly neighbours on the small council estate on Cathill where he lived and one or two mates in the tap room. His charges were low but he eschewed further business for obvious reasons. Father once asked him to mend some of the girls' school shoes which they seemed to wear out at a rapid rate, but he refused saying that there were plenty of shoemakers in the town. But on Saturday lunchtimes you would often see Charlie carrying a small brown paper parcel both on arriving at and leaving the Coach and Four.

One Saturday Seth Sagar, the Town Clerk, came in carrying a brown paper parcel. He ordered a drink from me and asked if Charlie Worth was in. I looked through the hatch and saw Charlie sitting in the corner contemplating his first pint of Best. I told Mister Sagar he was, and that worthy made what was generally reckoned to be his first ever visit to the tap room.

'Good morning Mister Worth, Good Morning gentlemen,' said the Town Clerk to the surprised occupants of the tap room. A series of slightly embarrassed grunts came in response, for whilst they knew Mister Sagar was a regular at the pub they hardly expected to be on social terms with him. He placed his glass of beer on Charlie's table and sat down.

Charlie was beginning to wonder how long it was since he had been called 'Mister Worth' when the Town Clerk handed him the parcel as if he was going through a regular practice. 'I wonder if you could kindly have these soled and heeled for me by next Saturday?' Charlie was taken aback and instead of his normal refusal he took the shoes and nodded his assent. Mister Sagar offered the room his comments on the weather and the local sporting scene, drank up his glass of beer and departed. The gentle hum of conversation gradually restarted.

The following Saturday Mister Sagar went straight to the tap room, which drew the remark from Alf Foyles that: 'He's beginning to be a regular in there.'

Charlie had the shoes neatly wrapped up and handed them over. Mister Sagar struck a confidential pose and quietly asked 'How much?'

Charlie said that no, it didn't matter, only too glad to do him a favour.

Pair of old boots

The Town Clerk insisted. He must pay Charlie something. The usual price was five shillings and perhaps a drink for Charlie. The Town Clerk persisted until Charlie, perturbed and embarrassed, gave in. 'OK then, Mister Sagar; give us a bob for each o' kids.'

They had several nommes de guerre. The 'Three Stooges' was the least polite; 'Tom, Dick and Harry' in no way reflected their correct handles but was useful if you had forgotten them; but the 'Three Wise Men' was the most common and that was the one that they liked to be known by. Not that they were wise, or stooges for that matter. Just three old mates, retired of course, who chose to meet together most days, talk about this and that and have a drink or two. They were mainly lunchtime drinkers and were seldom seen anywhere else other than the tap room of the Coach and Four or on the form outside looking across to the canal basin.

It was a suitable place to sit on sunny days for it faced due south. It was an appropriate place too because a small plaque on it recorded its dedication to 'George Horncastle, a regular of this public house for many years, died July, 1939. A gift from his colleagues in the tap room and the staff and management of the Coach and Four.' The Three Wise Men, or more properly, Albert, Big Bob and Little Bob, were amongst those who had subscribed for the seat and who held George Horncastle in happy memory.

There had always been a form outside the Coach and Four, in living memory at least. Who provided the first one isn't known but it was always accepted that the end nearest the pub door was reserved for George. In summer he would turn up around nine o'clock with the Daily Herald, read for a bit, maybe pick out a few winners which he never backed, and wait for his mates who in his latter years included the Three Wise Men. This was before the name became accepted, for no one would ever expect to outwise George Horncastle.

Little Bob told me of several incidents concerning him. He had an impish wit and didn't suffer fools gladly, particularly if they were strangers. About a quarter of a mile from the pub was a junc-

....

tion where the Calderthorpe road started its climb into that town and a valley road – known to all as 't'bottom road' wound its way towards denser parts of the West Riding. Motor cars were in their infancy and few were to be seen in this part of the country.

One pulled up outside the pub one morning and an aristocratic gent haughtily summoned George to the car. George ambled over to be asked: 'Is this the road to Calderthorpe?' to which George replied: 'Might be.'

He omitted to point out that the man had two choices. He was about to regain his seat when he driver spotted the junction. Slightly exasperated the man then demanded: 'Well, which of these roads leads to Calderthorpe?'

'Dunno,' said George.

'You don't know much do you?' said the now angry man.

'No,' said the sage of Oldford, 'but I'm not bloody well lost!'

He returned to his seat with some dignity.

Calderthorpe was always known to the inhabitants of Oldford as 'Up t'hill'. It was a simple geographic expression and saved folk the bother of pronouncing the extra syllable. Why use three when two would do. George Horncastle was an exponent of this economic form of speech. His answer to friends who asked the whereabouts of a particular person as he guarded the doorway to the pub was either: 'Yintin' (he is not in) or 'Sin' (he is in).

George enjoyed his self-appointed post of doorkeeper to the Coach and Four and he was encouraged in it by Old Jack the landlord of the day who relied upon him to keep an eye on things; to tell him the minor scandals of the town, who was banned from other pubs and who was credit worthy or not. George knew everything that happened in Oldford and everybody who lived there. If he didn't then he wanted to know why. Not that he was a know-all, anything but. He simply expected other folk to know as much as he did.

Another day and another car pulled up and again the driver wanted to know the way to Calderthorpe. This time one of George's mates answered the call. 'Was this the road to Calderthorpe?'

Taking his cue from George, although this driver was not as arrogant nor as rude as the previous one, he said he didn't know. What about the other way – t'bottom road. He didn't know that either. The driver left to find better information. He returned to his seat. 'Where did he want to go?' said George. 'Up t'hill,' said his mate. 'Well why the bloody hell didn't he say so?' snapped George.

The tap room was the heart of the pub. It was here where the characters resided and it was here that the various games teams were headquartered. There were three of them – darts, dominoes and fives-and-threes, and whilst the latter two were played with the same equipment their combatants were from different worlds, regarding their particular sport as far superior to the other. Apart from the dominoes and the pegging boards they had one other thing in common; they took themselves seriously. The darts team on the other hand was a joke.

The Oldford and District Darts and Dominoes League was an old established institution and its membership took in most of the pubs and clubs of the town and the surrounding villages. Dick Crabtree the landlord of the Pick and Shovel in Upper Darley was its president and one of the lads from his pub was ostensibly the secretary. Dick was a genial dictator and had been known to say more than once: '...democracy don't work... I'm in charge.' He arranged the fixtures, worked out the league tables, sorted out disputes between teams, organised the annual dinner and prize giving and, all round, did a fine job. Nobody complained and nobody else wanted the work.

The Coach and Four had teams in the first division of the dominoes and fives and threes leagues and in the fourth division of the darts league. This reflected the seriousness with which the teams treated their respective games. Each Monday evening the tap room would hum with activity. If the darts team was at home it would be rowdy with much laughter. They played for pleasure and other teams in the darts fourth division had a similar disposition and regretted that one or two of their ilk would have to be promoted at the end of the season.

It was expected that the landlord would occasionally travel to away matches and my father enjoyed the cut and thrust of the domino table, whatever game was being played and would some-times make up one of the teams. For my part I was a regular in the darts team's supporters club.

They were a bit like the rabbits at the golf club. The game was the least important part of the evening. What mattered was what went on afterwards. Each team did its own fund-raising to cover such things as travel costs, prizes and refreshments. In the senior leagues simple fare like sandwiches were perfectly acceptable but in the minor divisions the players, and supporters, looked for more substantial dishes and my mother became famous for her steak and kidney pies. Other pubs put on similar food: hot pot and pickles, black pudding with mustard and the Pick and Shovel was famous for its mince cobbler. Despite the lack of seriousness applied to the game there was never any shortage of players for the Coach and Four darts team.

We played a match at a working mens' club up the valley one cold winter's evening. Two taxis took the team and a couple of supporters there and we were welcomed by the secretary with the news that two of their team had been delayed by bad roads over into Lancashire but would we have a hot whisky whilst we waited – courtesy of the club. It seemed a pleasant enough gesture. Hot whisky is an import from Ireland and is made up of a shot of whisky of any variety and a similar quantity of boiling water with sugar, lemon and cloves. The intention is to keep out the cold rather than intoxicate. It was getting on for half past nine before the game got under way, the club's generosity had continued and both teams were almost drowning in hot whiskies.

One of the two late comers told me afterwards that he had never seen anything quite like it coming to the match as he did, stone cold sober. Players were having great difficulty hitting the board let alone making scores. Most games were a shambles and one lasted more than half an hour; the two late-coming sobersides felt obliged to lose their games and the only ever recorded tie in the history of the league was played that night. The rules stated that if the scores were equal after all six matches were played then each captain would nominate a player for a deciding match. This was done but, by just after midnight the home player still needed more than a hundred and our man had been trying to score double fifteen for nearly ten minutes. The taxi drivers, tired of

Players were having great difficulty hitting the board

waiting, were threatening to leave us. It was decided to call it a draw but not before arranging a follow-up friendly.

Another match, at home this time, happened to coincide with a game in the domino league. Their seriousness was often over portrayed for, on the whole, they were a decent bunch, a bit older than the darts players, who would let their hair down at what they called 'the proper time'. The trouble was that the darts players made a lot of noise. A complaint from the domino team captain was met with the suggestion that they could move to the snug to play but that was rejected as women were watching television in there and, in any case, why should they?

Into the evening it became obvious that 'crabbed age and youth can't play darts and dominoes together' as Norman Dyson put it. One member of the visiting domino team was very nearly spiked by a dart bouncing off a wire, a complete accident as it happened. He was furious, slammed down his dominoes and walked out. This led to an almighty row with accusations both between players in the different games and from the different pubs. Fortunately the good nature of the darts players shone through and they cleared the tap room to allow the domino match to finish.

Ours wasn't an isolated incident and there were other examples of the various games and divisions failing to get on. Dick Crabtree sorted things out. He had heard about the problems and decided that the darts league should be moved to Tuesdays to avoid any more tap room clashes. Objections – 'why should we change?' – were muted and soon snuffed. Dick had spoken.

🍺 🍺 🍺 🍺 🍺 🍺 🍺 🍺 🍺 🍺

Women were rare in the tap room. It wasn't that they were banned or even not made welcome. But the men who used it regarded it as their province where the odd swear word wasn't held back or rebuked when issued. The older men in particular felt more at home there and their wives often said that they seemed to have more time for them (the wives) when they returned from a session. Women, in any case, had their own room in the snug at the back of the pub.

But anyone who thought it was exclusively a mens' club reckoned without Annie and Polly. The weekend that they came to stay at the Coach and Four was remembered in Oldford for many a long day, maybe even to today. They were friends of mine; we had been at the same teacher training college and renewed our acquaintanceship at a class reunion.

The two had always been the bright stars of our group, full of humour and bursting with personality. Annie lived where she had always lived in North Yorkshire and was teaching in a comprehensive school on Teesside. Polly came from 'darn sarf' as she called it but was teaching in Northern Ireland. They were both good lookers but had no attachments and were putting their careers first for the time being at least. When they learned that I was living in a pub they promptly invited themselves for the half term holiday.

My mother raised the usual objections. Who were they? What was I doing with two girl friends? I pointed out that I hadn't even got one girl friend, working in a school all day and at a pub most evenings and weekends didn't give a lot of time for romance. She was justified of course in suggesting that I ought to have consulted her first before issuing the invite but I could hardly explain that I had had little to do with it. Annie and Polly had decided they were coming.

Came the day and I drove to Preston to meet Polly off the boat train and together we hopped back across the Pennines to Skipton to pick up Annie. They seemed to have enough luggage for six and my poor little pre-war Morris Ten had to struggle up the hills out of Keighley. We made it and the girls made whooping noises about 'the delightful pub' and 'the quaint town'. Delightful the pub may have been but Oldford was anything but quaint. The trouble with these two was that while I thought I understood their sense of humour I was concerned that nobody else might.

However my parents, and my mother in particular, seemed to get on fine with them. She gave them a large room on the top floor and ordered my sisters, who were still chattering on about them being my two girl friends, to give a hand with the luggage and see that the visitors had everything they wanted. Mother prepared one of her usual enormous meals, making the point that both girls looked as though they 'needed feeding up'. It being a Saturday, visitors or not, I had to work.

My father however was sensitive to my situation. If I opened up the pub at five o' clock I could knock off about nine and enjoy the rest of the evening with my guests. Jimmy Machin who had also been at college with us and lived in Leeds was coming over for the evening. By the time nine o' clock arrived I was ready for a drink but singularly unprepared for my guests.

I asked my father where the girls were and he pointed to the tap room. I shrugged my shoulders and went in. There they were with pints of Best in front of them holding court to the dozen or so middle aged and elderly blokes who regularly frequented the place. A few younger ones had also drifted in and were hovering around the dart board with no real interest in the game but with plenty in the visitors.

Annie was telling a tale of how she had lost all her luggage when she went on a bus trip across North America. She was putting it on a bit. 'All I had left,' she said 'was what I stood up in and a spare pair of knickers in my handbag. I always carry them, you never know when you might need them.'

....

Polly stepped in to cap her friend. Her story was of the day her clothes got stolen while she was bathing off the coast of Donegal. 'There I was,' she said 'in just my bikini and not even any mad money to pay my bus fare home.'

Several of the chaps wanted to know how she managed it.

'Called the old bill,' she declared, 'and asked them for a lift home while they caught the blighter who nicked my clobber.'

They were tales I had heard several times before and I was never quite sure how true they were although I suspect there was some degree of veracity in them. Both were adventurous lasses and quite likely to get up to the sort of mischief they were relating. It occurred to me that I had never heard the ending of either story.

'Did you ever get your clothes back, Polly?' I asked. 'Or your luggage, Annie?'

'Drinks anyone?' said Jimmy Machin intervening at an apposite moment.

'Two pints of Best, it's good to drink some decent beer again,' said Polly looking round for confirmation from the regulars and getting it. They would have agreed if she had told them it was alcohol free.

They had the place in a trance. When I suggested a walk out to one or two other pubs I got some cold stares and little support from my friends, 'Tomorrow,' pronounced Annie. It was a state-ment of intent and not a point to discuss. Tomorrow it was to be.

For the rest of the evening we had an uproarious time and father had something of a job to clear the tap room at closing time. He declared that he had never taken as much money in that room on a Saturday night. I said it was because of the girls.

'You ought to invite us back regularly Mister Lowe,' said Polly.

'Not a bad idea; but call me Alex,' said father, falling under their spell.

🍺 🍺 🍺 🍺 🍺 🍺 🍺 🍺 🍺 🍺

The tap room crowd decided to run a football pool syndicate. It allowed them to send in a complicated mass entry and while it reduced the possible amount of winnings it increased their chances. That was how the theory went. But, of course, it wasn't as simple as that. First of all someone had to collect the money and someone had to look after it and send in the coupon each week.

'What about you, Wilf?' said Charlie Worth, one of the regulars.

'No fear,' I said knowing my inability to manage my own finances let alone anyone else's. 'But, if you find someone to fill in the coupon, I'm sure dad will be the treasurer.'

In fact I knew he would. That's if he agreed with the idea of a syndicate for he took the view that vanishing funds did no good for a pub whoever was responsible. He had seen enough of money going missing when he worked in the club trade in Lancashire what with a Christmas club treasurer doing a moonlight flit a month before the payout and the organiser of a football sweep gambling the proceeds away and trying to say that he'd left three weeks takings on a bus while on his way to the bank to pay them in.

Tim Massey a retired railway clerk was the obvious man to collect the money, select the entries and send in the coupon. He was a regular and popular with all in the tap room, secretary of the domino team and football daft. He was however, slightly nervous, a little deaf and inclined to stutter a bit. Occasionally he mixed up his words.

Once when confronted by a policeman who merely posed the rhetorical question 'nice day?' he broke into a sweat and mumbled something like 'it wasn't me officer'. Another time he called the Town Clerk, the 'clown turk'. But he recognised his faults and joked that sometimes he was troubled by a 'tip of the slongue'.

My father agreed to hold the money, sign the cheques and, he joked, pay out the dividends. The sum agreed was one shilling each week and there were some twenty-odd members including me as an honorary tap room user. Otherwise it was strictly limited to those who frequented the room regularly.

Tim came in for a bit of stick each week from his fellow members. 'Have you got Preston Both Ends down for a draw?' he would be ribbed.

'Clapton Ornaments are a banker,' he was advised. And so on. He took it in good grace and sometimes threw it back.

'Hamilton Accidentals let us down last week,' said Tim. 'That's the last time I'll listen to your tips, Charlie Worth.'

But they persisted and half a dozen times in that first season we had some minor dividends. Usually it was ploughed back into the kitty along with the small weekly surplus; once or twice it paid out a pound or two to each member.

Came the last week of the domestic season and I was away with some of the sixth formers on a weekend holiday climbing in north Wales. I got back late on Monday evening not having seen the football results and the old man said: 'Great news, son, we've got a first dividend on the pools.'

'How much?' I demanded.

'We don't know yet until the cheque comes on Wednesday.' I would have to be patient.

At morning break on Wednesday I was on the phone to my father. 'How much?'

'Hold your breath,' he said. 'We've got one first dividend, six seconds, 24 thirds, 60 fourths and the Lord knows how many fifths.

'HOW MUCH?' I yelled, frightening the rest of the staff room.

My father's reply was to the point: 'You won't have to pay for the first two weeks of next season.'

I had been set up again. That week there were 28 draws – a record and practically everybody who entered expected something. The first dividend was two pounds and there were no smaller ones.

CHAPTER 5

······························

THE LANDLORD'S TALE

"Any idiot can make beer come out of a tap. You've got to be a psychologist to do this job."
ANONYMOUS PUB LANDLORD

IT SEEMED OUR PUB HAD A GHOST. Few people had actually seen it but there were plenty who would witness to its presence in one way or another. Looking back I suspect that quite a few of these experiences were due to an excess of drink. The Christmas brew of Old Ale had a lot to answer for and many of Harrison's landlords only sold it in half pints or even by the 'pony' – the authentic gill or quarter of a pint.

But I was interested and I started to document the various sightings, hearings and other phenomena. The one that interested me most was that of Wendy, my youngest sister. For the first time in their lives my sisters had separate bedrooms. Wendy had a large corner room with a connecting door to a store room that may at one time have been a dressing room. The store was full of lumber, some left by previous landlords and some brought by us, including two tea chests full of my books.

One night mother heard Wendy scream and on rushing to her room found her distraught and crying and saying that she had heard voices in the store room. Father inspected the room but nothing extraordinary could be found there but, for the girl's peace of mind, she spent the rest of the night with her sister. A couple of days later I talked to them both and tried to convince them that there was no such thing as a ghost. What Wendy heard could be explained by natural events. She may have believed me but she said she had heard noises in the room before and she was still rather frightened. Eventually she moved into another room.

Conversation in the pub brought to light other stories but there did seem to be a link to that small store room. Norman had slept in the corner bedroom several times over the years when he had had too much to drink to risk driving his car home. He told me that he had heard noises like something heavy being dragged across the floor. But he once found a pigeon in there that had come out of the rafters and through a hole made by damp in the corner of the ceiling. Perhaps, he thought, other such birds might have been responsible. Perhaps they were what Wendy had heard.

Father called in the sanitary inspectors and they examined the roof void and brought out a dozen or so dead birds and discovered they had got in through some damaged slates. These were replaced and the hole in the ceiling was mended.

Two weeks later my cousin, Colin, from Sheffield stayed one weekend and slept in the corner room. He was woken on both nights by what he thought were voices and heavy objects being moved about. He was a sturdy soul and proclaimed that it didn't bother him but I got the impression that he was slightly apprehensive about the whole business and possibly also a little drunk. It was some time before he came again.

One of the regulars, George Wright, remembered a different ghost, or at least 'the ghost' operating in a different part of the pub. It had happened years before, around 1938 when he was a painter and decorator and the then landlord, Old Jack, had employed him to decorate the public rooms of the Coach and Four. It was a big job and to cut inconvenience to a minimum the work was done overnight in several stages. The concert room, tap room and snug were finished and work had just started on the biggest section, the bar and the large hallway.

George had his son and another man helping him. On the night in question the pub had been cleared quickly and they set to work. 'It was just after midnight,' said George. 'I was standing on the bar counter putting lining paper on the ceiling when I felt this movement of very cold air pass me going towards the back of the pub. The other two felt it as well and there was no obvious explanation for it.'

He went on to say that he would have thought no more about it but while he was on leave from the army around 1944 he happened to overhear a customer say that 'Old Jack was getting a bit worried about his ghost'. He inquired and learned that the landlord had felt a draught of cold air several times, usually about midnight, usually moving to the back of the pub. George spoke to the landlord and they agreed that their experiences had been similar, but George went back to the forces and when he returned to civilian life 'Old Jack' had retired to Scarborough.

I tried to find out if anyone else knew anything about our ghost. Had anyone seen it? One man claimed to have done but his capacity for strong drink was not matched by his capacity to maintain sobriety. What he had to say however fitted in with other folks' tales. Again it was around midnight on a night when our boozy friend and a few others had been 'locked in' as the saying goes. Most of them felt the draught but he swore he saw the grey figure of a man move towards the cellar door which was at the back of the pub. No one else confirmed the sighting.

I was told Old Jack's widow now lived in Leeds with her daughter. I contacted the daughter and asked if her mother, aged 80, would agree to see me. She said she would be pleased to but didn't think she would remember a lot about it. In her own room at the back of an airy semi-detached in Headingley I spoke to her about 'Jack's ghost' as she called it. She remembered the wartime incidents and had even felt the cold draught herself once or twice but she hadn't seen anything. And then, without any prompting from me, she said she thought a room on the second floor might be haunted. 'Which one?' I asked anxiously. 'The big one in the corner on the left with a little dressing room off it.' It was what had been Wendy's room.

She told me that for a while during the war they had troops billeted on them, usually convalescing from injuries and often from foreign countries; France, Poland, later the United States. The whole of the top floor was used and housed around twelve servicemen. The corner room slept three with another one in the box room. It was in here that a Polish airman had committed suicide.

'Poor lad,' she said, slightly distressed by the memory of the incident. 'He wasn't very happy, hadn't many friends and the other lads complained that he used to talk in his sleep and was always moving things around. Then one morning he didn't come down for breakfast and one of the others found him hanging by a cord from the roof beams.'

But what made her think the room was haunted despite this unfortunate event? It turned out that she had gone in there once or twice after the troops had left when they were using it as a store, and felt what she described as 'a presence'. She couldn't explain it but was certain there was something there.

I had been there for more than two hours, the old lady was getting tired, so I decided not to tell her about the other events concerning the small room, thanked her and left. The following day I sent her some flowers and phoned her daughter to make sure the visit hadn't been too much for her mother.

It had to be done of course and I had to do it. I decided to combine both events, to sit in an empty pub at midnight and then sleep in the corner room. Brian Dyson suggested I should spend a night in the small room. I rejected this suggestion but I did persuade him to sit up with me for the first part of the evening. We saw the family off to bed and settled down to enjoy a pint or two of Harrison's Best.

To say we felt a cold draught would put it a bit strong. But at thirteen minutes into that Tuesday morning, Brian Dyson and Wilf Lowe both shivered. I put it no greater an experience than that. So we had a couple of large whiskies, I let Brian out and took my tentative steps to the corner room.

It was a cosy room and in other circumstances I would have enjoyed staying there. The view was over the canal basin to Dogwood Fell and even at night was a pleasant one with the burnished roofs of the warehouses glistening in the moonlight and the odd street light picking out the moorland roads. Would that I felt as placid.

I read for a while in my usual custom but my mind wasn't on Priestley's 'Good Companions'. So I attempted to sleep. For some reason I had it in my mind that if I remained awake nothing would happen but I had had a busy day both at school and in the pub, and it was late. I slept, if not the sleep of the just, then something closely approaching it.

At half past seven the two girls rushed into the room demanding to know what had happened and were greatly disappointed to find that I had not heard, let alone seen anything. The family consensus was that I had drunk too much and would have slept through a thunder storm.

Later we had a lodger, Dave Stephens, who used the room two or three times a week. He was from London and was the sales manager of a firm connected with the textile trade and spent a lot of time in the area. We gathered his domestic affairs were a bit awry but we asked nothing and he offered nothing. He always paid on the dot for a full week; he enjoyed our company and we his. It was a good arrangement. Dave was always telling my mother what a comfortable room it was and how well he slept there. I was under penalty of something just short of death to mention anything to him about our 'ghost'.

🍺 🍺 🍺 🍺 🍺 🍺 🍺 🍺 🍺 🍺

Old Jack had been the landlord of the Coach and Four through the war years. His only son – Young Jack – who now kept a pub in Bradford had served as a sergeant in the West Yorkshire Regiment with some distinction, being mentioned in dispatches on two occasions. His parents were very proud of him. Came the end of the war and his return from Italy was awaited with great excitement.

During that period of late 1945 into 1946 'welcome home' signs were to be seen all over Oldford. Houses were painted with the crosses of the Union Jack; red, white and blue bunting was stretched across streets; and when one local hero who had won the Military Medal came home the Oldford Prize Band was there to greet him.

But for many returning servicemen their arrival in the town was something of a surprise. Often they were given leave at a moment's notice and off they would go on the first train available from wherever they may be stationed to Leeds or Manchester, then connecting to Oldford. There was no time to let their families know.

The Oldford Prize Band was there to greet him

The landlady of the Coach and Four decided to go one better than the rest of the town to welcome back her son. She made a flag from a large bed sheet on which she patiently embroidered 'Welcome Home Jack!' She attached this to a clothes prop and wedged it through the first floor window overlooking the front door. It flew there for around three weeks before Young Jack received his welcome.

Jack's battalion had returned from Italy to barracks on Salisbury Plain. As soon as they were settled in, batches of them were sent off for a week's leave. Jack was one of the first. He got the news around four o'clock one afternoon. He quickly packed a bag, stored the rest of his gear, collected a travel warrant from the company office and hot footed it to Tisbury station for a train to Waterloo.

From there he took the underground to St Pancras and just managed to catch the mail train to Leeds. It arrived there in the early hours and connected with a local to Calderthorpe which stopped at Oldford. He considered himself very lucky so far. By the time he reached the Coach and Four it was just beginning to show daylight. He knocked on the door and it was some minutes before he could wake anyone up.

Old Jack opened the first floor window to see who was knocking them up at that unearthly hour. The prop, weighted down by the flag, tipped up and plummeted to the ground. It struck Young Jack full on the forehead and laid him out cold. Old Jack and his wife rushed downstairs and opened the door to find Young Jack flat out on the pavement covered with the flag proclaiming: 'Welcome Home Jack.'

When we lived in Lancashire I had a dog called Whisky. It was an average sized mongrel with an aptitude for survival. It had its own patch at the bottom of our large back garden and could hold its own with most of the other curs that roamed the streets of our estate. The move posed problems for Whisky even if he were not aware of them.

Because I was moving, albeit temporarily, into digs, the best solution seemed to be for my folks to take the dog to the pub and that was what happened. My sisters after showing initial reluctance agreed to look after him when I offered to pay what they called wages and what I called blackmail. Whisky knew he was in good hands. He became a popular figure around the pub but was soon showing signs of fattening up due to being indulged by the customers and, in my view, because of lack of exercise from my sisters. They denied it and pointed out, quite rightly, though I was not prepared to admit this, that he was not allowed to roam as freely as before because of the busy main road at the front of the pub.

All went well until about ten weeks after the move. I arrived at the Coach and Four one Saturday morning having been to a union meeting the previous evening. Mother was visibly upset and told me that Whisky had gone missing. No one could understand why, how or when. But Norman Dyson had a theory.

The previous night a coach trip had called at the pub around nine o'clock with a mixed party of about 30. They had been to York races and were pub crawling it back to Manchester. Ours was their last stop. They had a noisy but good-tempered evening and father was well satisfied with the amount that went through the till. Two or three of the younger men had been feeding Whisky with crisps and it was with these lads that anyone last remembered seeing the dog.

Norman believed they had enticed Whisky on to the coach for what they, in their semi-drunken state, might have regarded as a joke. From then on anything could have happened. The more sober folk on the bus might have remonstrated with them and he could have been taken to someone's home and might be living a perfectly happy life. Knowing Whisky I imagined that he would settle down quickly with a new owner. On the other hand the dog might have been released somewhere between Oldford and Manchester and could be anywhere.

However, I was very upset for I had great affection for the dog and I questioned many people in my attempts to trace him. Nobody remembered the name of the coach company or which part of Manchester it had come from. The local police were helpful but reluctant to do very much, mainly because there was no hard evidence that the dog had been taken away by the Manchester coach party.

I continued my enquiries and obtained a list of coach companies in the Manchester area and commenced phoning round. At least six had sent coaches to York races on that day and whilst a couple offered to ask their drivers if they had stopped at the Coach and Four on the return journey there was no great enthusiasm and most displayed an attitude of indifference – a lost dog is a lost dog. None of them returned my call.

Three weeks later the main domestic news of the day was of an outbreak of foot and mouth disease in the north of England. Amongst other things local authorities did their bit by rounding up stray animals. I was having my evening meal and watching the local news on my landlady's newly acquired television. It showed a dog pound in the Manchester area with dozens of assorted hounds barking what appeared to be a welcome to the television cameraman. At the front, a natural leader, was Whisky. To me, he was unmistakable.

All I knew was that it was in Manchester. I rang the BBC and got pushed around from department to department. The producer had gone home; the cameraman was a freelance; no they couldn't give me any telephone numbers, it was against BBC policy; why not try again tomorrow. It was frustrating because the implication was given by the television reporter that pretty soon all the stray dogs would be destroyed.

The following morning I had a free period and the school secretary gave me free rein on the phone and even did some chasing herself. We contacted the producer who fortunately had his eye on the main chance and recognised the possibility of a good follow-up story. He promised to go back to the pound to try and rescue Whisky. I phoned home to see if my father could get over there as well. Of course the BBC man had no idea what the dog looked liked but I impressed on him to call out 'Whisky' and the mutt would come running. And that is precisely what happened. Shortly afterwards father arrived and the whole reunion scene was filmed.

Whisky went home to an ecstatic welcome from family and pub customers and eventually, two days later, from me. The BBC decided not to use the piece but the producer sold the story to one of the tabloids, which made a great show of 'Little Dog Lost – and Found'. We never did discover who took him away but Whisky led a much more confined life afterwards particularly when there were coach parties about.

🍺 🍺 🍺 🍺 🍺 🍺 🍺 🍺 🍺 🍺

My father received a letter containing a card which read: The Mayor of Oldford (Councillor Alfred Percival Hetherington, JP) requests the pleasure of Mr Alexander Lowe at 3.30 p.m. on Thursday, 7 June, in the Mayor's Parlour, Town Hall, Oldford. Tea will be served. RSVP.

'What is it?' asked my mother.

'It's from Alfie,' said my father, 'he wants me to go for tea with him.'

Alfie Hetherington was a regular at the Coach and Four and at most of the other pubs and clubs in Oldford with the sole exception of the Conservative Club. He was an engine driver, a stalwart trade unionist and a pillar of the Labour Party. His frequent visits to the town's pubs and clubs were a matter of pleasure for him for it was said, and he never denied it, that he got most of his votes from them. Alfie, folk said, didn't need to canvass he just needed to walk round the pubs. His popularity was undoubted.

He was serving his second spell as Mayor of the town and the acceptance of this high office made no inroads on his boozing. On more than one occasion he came into the Coach and Four in full mayoral regalia with his chauffeur cum attendant after parking the official Rolls Royce outside the pub. He would have been to some do or other and felt the need as he said: '…for a decent pint after all that wine.'

On one occasion during his first mayoralty minor royalty came to Oldford to open a new hospital. 'The Duke and Duchess of somewhere' as Alfie put it. He was relatively young and inexperienced at the time, the town's youngest ever Mayor. He chatted amiably to the Duchess during the lunch that followed the opening but was a little worried as to how he should address the royal personage in his speech. Plucking up courage he decided to ask her directly.

'I think you should carry on calling me "love" like you've been doing for the past twenty minutes,' she replied.

We all liked Alfie and dad was delighted, if not a little puzzled, to have received the invitation. Off he went and found most of his fellow licensees were present along with a smattering of the town's businessmen and representatives of its social life. Tea and scones were passed around and eventually the Mayor asked everybody to take a seat and started the meeting. What he wanted to do, he said, was to put Oldford on the map. He felt the town ought to have a big event that would stand alongside the big shows of the country towns, with the music festivals of the industrial cities and with the feasts and fairs all over the county. 'Oldford,' declared the Mayor in his indomitable fashion, 'has nowt!'

My father said it was an interesting meeting and the town clerk, Seth Sagar – another of our regulars – had obviously given the idea a lot of thought. His proposal was, for the want of a better word, to have a big 'do' in September in which all facets of Oldford life would be displayed. Also there ought to be a lot of fun. The spin-off might be something for the Mayor's charity but in the first year that wasn't important. Working groups were formed and licensees were one of them – father, never one to say No, was its chairman.

They met at the pub one afternoon in the following week. Bert Cox made the point that there were more present than they got at Licensed Victuallers Association meetings. Ideas were tossed around and in the end they came up with the plan of a team race around the pubs of Oldford with prizes given by the landlords and collections for charity on the way round. It was knocked about a bit with customers at the various pubs throwing in their ideas but on the whole everybody seemed to think it would work and be a useful addition to what was becoming known as 'Alfie's Do!'

The final arrangement was that it would be a bed race with a girl on the bed and four blokes to propel and carry it around the town. They would make calls at ten pubs in any order they wished where all five would either drink a half pint of beer or a glass of milk or eat an apple before moving on. The canal would have to be crossed twice at different points and whilst the bridge opposite our pub was an obvious choice, returning was more difficult. It either meant a mile slog to the lock and back or swimming across. Supporters would have collecting boxes and there would be prizes for the fastest times – the starts being staggered – and for the best get-up.

I was told to take charge of the entry for the Coach and Four. Selecting the four men was no problem with Bernard Lynn, Brian Dyson, Eric Smithies and me, but finding a lady who would allow herself to be dragged around town on a bed by four rowdy young men was another thing particularly after Brian said that with it being a bed she must wear a shortie nightie. We asked Mary but Norman put his foot down and my mother blocked the attempts of my younger sister Wendy to volunteer. Eventually Eric's wife Julia agreed but said it was against her better judgement and in no circumstances was she wearing a short nightdress.

Our event was, of course, just one of many that made up 'Alfie's

Do'. There was a big parade in the morning with all the various local organisations taking part led off by the Oldford Prize Band. No one was ever quite sure what prize they had won but the name had stuck. Marching through the town were scouts, guides, the St John Ambulance Brigade, Boys Brigade, WVS, Territorials, bed race competitors, yes even our lot got in on the act. Open topped lorries carried floats from voluntary and commercial organisations – the Co-operative Society, the Red Cross, banks, young farmers, the League of Health and Beauty and even British Rail had a Victorian shunting engine on the back of one of their wagons.

It was a fine parade and Alfie, the Mayor, proudly took the salute as it passed the Town Hall. The populace turned out in force, shops and buildings were decorated, all the pubs had day-long extensions and there was a full programme of events through the day culminating in a fireworks display and what the Mayor chose to call a Grand Balls-up!

The Bed Race started at two o'clock from the Oldford Town football club's ground. The teams left at five minute intervals to avoid clogging up the roads. There were 35 entries and we went off at half past two. Our team 'colours' were yellow and green shirts which Vera Brocklesby had dashed up for us and the bed displayed a sign: 'The Coach and Four Canaries'. It was a splendid old bed given to us by a customer of the pub and it had brass knobs and, fortunately, a full set of castors. The parade had been useful in helping us to learn how to manoeuvre with Julia on board and we felt very confident.

Our first stop was the Dog and Duck where we all had glasses of milk. This was a deliberate decision on our part. We agreed to have milk for most of the stops interspersed with the odd apple or two and finishing with a couple of halves of beer. This, we reckoned, had the advantage of keeping our strength up and not getting us too full or too intoxicated. We hoped. Our plan was to work our way to the west end of town and cross the canal at the lock then down the tow path to the bridge. The Coach and Four and the George were the next stops and then it was back into the town centre with the last call being at the Big Crown and up to the football ground. It should take about an hour and a half. All the pubs were prepared, with tables outside them with full glasses and apples ready for the teams. We grabbed, drank or ate, and off we went to the next stop.

Our route was longer than the way most of the others chose but it was the drier way, so we thought. The short way was to cross the bridge and then, after visiting a couple of pubs on the south side of town, manhandle the bed across the canal. It saved a mile but it meant all four men, and almost certainly the girl, getting wet.

We made it to the lock and only then realised how difficult it was going to be to get the bed with Julia on board to the other side. There was only room for one man at each end of the bed on the lock gate catwalk. Bernard and Eric were the biggest and they started across with encouragement from Brian and I. Halfway across we tried to help by taking over from them. I managed to get a hold on the bed and Bernard got behind me but Brian was having problems taking over from Eric. They got into a right muddle and despite efforts from our end we could see the bed tilting and Julia slipping off. And into the canal she went – Splash!

We dragged her out and cheated a little by pulling the bed across without her on it. Our intention to dash on down the tow path was thwarted by Julia who screamed at us that we were not only so many thousand fools, idiots and dolts but that she wasn't moving an inch until she had dried out. Some of our supporters came to the rescue by lending pieces of their clothing and the girls surrounded Julia's modesty to allow her to dry off and change. We were on our way again.

The tow path was tough going but we made it, then, after the two south side pubs, we went over the bridge at the canal basin across the road to the Coach and Four where I had my first beer. I could have managed a gallon but there were still four other pubs to call at. We moved on with leaden feet but enjoying ourselves none the less. At last we sank our final drink – in my case a pint – at the Big Crown and slogged it up the hill to the finish. We were knackered, to say the least, but very happy and our time put us in the early lead. Bob Smithies had organised the return of the bed and the rest of us jumped into cars and drove back to the pub for a few well-deserved pints. At least that was our view.

The rest of the day was a bit of a haze. We were full of ourselves and certainly Brian and I weren't fit to work. I vaguely remember going across to the George for a pint and then back to the Big Crown where the results were being compiled. The atmosphere was tremendous and when the results were announced there was loud cheering for every winner. We won a prize of two gallons of beer for being the best turned out team and in the race we came third and won five sets of sheets and pillowcases.

Later that evening after the 'Grand Balls-up' the Mayor came into the boisterous atmosphere of the Coach and Four. He was in full regalia and seemed to have most of the town council including Seth Sagar the Town Clerk with him. None of them seemed very sober but then, neither were we. 'It's our last stop Alex,' Alfie told my father, 'so don't throw us out.'

The sight of the Mayor of Oldford in ermine and scarlet robes with his gold chain around his neck, sitting drinking pints of bitter with his stockinged feet up on a stool confirmed my faith in the democratic processes of British local government. Of course he got a late drink, after all he was also the chief magistrate of the town!

The toilets were badly in need of redecoration. The gents in particular were in a poor state. The walls had been painted in a ghastly green, the sort you find on school railings. It had started to peel and some joker had played about with and widened a hole to look something like a map of Australia. Names of towns were written such as Sydney, Brisbane, Darwin and Perth. Then another piece of paint was scratched out to become Tasmania. This was followed by Papua New Guinea and then New Zealand. It became something of a cult.

About a mile up the Calderthorpe road was the local teacher training college. Many of the students used the pub and some of them had worked for us as waiters. On the whole they were a pleasant enough crowd and my own recent experience made me sympathetic to them. I knew what it was like to be away from home and broke. The old man wouldn't allow tick but he did cash cheques for those he knew and he gave work out on what he called a 'work for need' basis. 'I'm waiting for my grant cheque Mister Lowe, how about a couple of nights work?' He picked the reliable ones and refused work to those who might have been stuck for cash but who were hard into their examinations.

Of course he got a late drink,
after all he was the chief magistrate

The students union usually organised events to welcome new students arriving for the winter term and allow them to get to know the town. In our first year at the pub they arranged a treasure hunt around the local pubs. It involved teams of two or three students visiting eight pubs and answering three questions about each of them. It would finish at one of the larger pubs where they would have supper and a few drinks and the prizes would be presented.

There wasn't much in it for the first seven pubs but most competitors would have a quick drink whilst solving the clues. Some of the groups were a bit secretive but it was obvious what they were involved in. Others would simply ask the staff the questions posed to them. The three questions for the Coach and Four were fairly simple. One asked the price of a measure of Irish Whiskey, which was a trick because it wasn't sold there; the second asked the name of the landlord and those who failed to inquire and wrote down the name above the door would get it wrong because it had not yet been changed to my father's. The third simply said: 'Where is Australia?'

Father was in the bar and amused himself by helping out the ones who bought drinks and being cussed to those who didn't. Politeness also counted with him. There came a run of half a dozen groups who failed both my father's tests – they didn't buy drinks and weren't very polite. After about three of them had demanded to know where Australia was he said to me: 'I'm fed up with this lot not buying drinks, I'll show them where Australia is.' And off he went upstairs to return at once with a paint scraper.

He went straight into the gents and scratched off the surrounding paint around Australia to leave it looking more like the Pacific Ocean. In came the next group who not only bought pints but after sorting out the first two questions were polite enough to ask my father if he could help them. 'Australia,' he said, 'is in the gent's toilet but there's no point in going to look for it, because it's gone.' They looked puzzled but took his word for it and went off to the next pub. 'I hope you win,' said father.

The next three groups all got father's back up and left not only failing to find out where the sub continent was – 'Australia,' said father, 'never heard of it. Don't know what you're on about.' – but also imagining that the landlord's name was Titchener, that of the previous tenant and still recorded above the door. The last groups got what information they asked for according to father's criteria.

The young man from the student's union who had organised the treasure hunt came round a few nights later to thank all the licensees for their trouble and patience. He was curious why so few had got the question right about Australia. In the absence of father

I explained what had happened and he was most amused, saying it served the mean beggars right. The whole idea, he said, was to let freshers get to know the local pubs and dashing in and out of them did them no good and only annoyed the landlords and their staffs. I bought him a drink and he said that the next one would be organised to finish at the Coach and Four. I said that I would arrange for a map of Australia to be hung in the ladies!

🍺 🍺 🍺 🍺 🍺 🍺 🍺 🍺 🍺 🍺

Charity, as they say, begins at home. But pubs are expected to take the lead in raising funds, particularly for local good causes. In the time we were at the Coach and Four most pub counters sported a collecting box for a local church building fund, a hospital or a youth club. Quite a few had Christmas stockings for the Fire Services National Benevolent Fund, or the Bent Elephant fund as the firemen who collected them called it. Our box was for the local Methodist church that organised Christmas parcels for needy old folk. We also supported the Salvation Army whose members visited the pub every Saturday night collecting and selling the War Cry and the Young Soldier. The games teams would occasionally run a raffle for some worthy cause and no reasonable request to collect in the pub was refused by my father. We were no different to many other pubs in our efforts.

My sisters had been selling tickets for a raffle organised at their school for the Save the Children Fund. Their innocent looking faces had persuaded many customers to buy tickets and they were quite delighted with their efforts. Father had given a bottle of whisky to the prize fund and much to everybody's delight it was won by one of the regulars and so were a couple of other prizes. My mother was pleased by the way the girls had worked hard at selling tickets and decided to run her own raffle for the Christmas parcel scheme run by the Methodist church. We weren't Methodists but it was so obviously a good idea that mother reckoned she could do a good job for it.

The girls went along with it and agreed to sell tickets – indeed they were the backbone of the organisation. Father set about obtaining prizes. Mary Dyson managed to secure a weekend for two in London from the travel agency she worked for; Jack Thornton from the brewery offered two crates of beer; Norman Dyson gave a suit length of top quality cloth and my parents put up a case of wine. It was going well. The darts team held a preliminary raffle to raise money to buy prizes and the other teams felt obliged to do something similar. A large blackboard displayed the growing list of prizes and ticket sales were booming.

The local Methodist minister was a pleasant young chap with a delightful wife and they both had none of the inhibitions usually associated with their denomination so far as drink was concerned. Not that they were boozers, but because of the efforts of my mother for their fund, what drink they took was usually in the Coach and Four. Mother asked them to come along and draw the raffle and they were pleased to do so. It was held on a Friday in late November and we made something of an evening of it. One of the regulars, Ronnie Taylor, did his stint on the piano, sandwiches were laid on and there was a festive atmosphere. The girls were allowed to stay up and tickets were selling merrily in all rooms. At about nine o'clock they stopped to allow the stubs to be separated and folded for the draw. The British Legion club had loaned father the large drum it used for weekly raffles.

The Methodist minister made a very witty speech thanking everybody for their efforts and saying what a good cause the money was going to.

My youngest sister, Wendy the uninhibited one, presented him with a cheque for £150 saying, amidst laughter, that '...there's more to come.'

Then the draw, and the minister read out the winners: 'First Prize, a weekend for two in London, ticket bought by Mister Alex Lowe, the Coach and Four, Oldford.'

There was uproar and shouts of 'Fix!' followed by laughter.

'Redraw it,' said my father.

'Cheers,' said the crowd.

Off went the minister again: 'First Prize, weekend in London, winner: Mary Dyson, Calderthorpe Travel, Regent Street, Calderthorpe.'

The shouts of 'Fix!' were even louder as everybody knew from the blackboard that Calderthorpe Travel had donated the prize.

Of course, Mary asked for it to be drawn again and this time it went to one of the customers who accepted it despite the continuing cries of 'Fix!'

The fun continued when I won a voucher for a box of fruit given by the local greengrocer but instead of asking for it to be drawn again I passed it on to the minister for his fund.

And then all went well until the final prize of the evening, a sack of coal, for which the minister drew out his own ticket.

The cries of 'fix' were at their loudest and despite efforts on his part to give it back he was persuaded, indeed ordered by my mother, to keep it. The evening had been a great success, eventually we raised £200 and from then on it became an annual event looked forward to with pleasure by the pub regulars and recipients alike.

My father was called up to the brewery in Calderthorpe to see John Harrison, the managing director, and our area manager, Jack Thornton, about some alterations the brewery wanted to make at the Coach and Four. The idea was that the back snug would go to be replaced by a modern kitchen and the toilets would be extended and refurbished. Most people in the pub wanted to keep the snug – the 'ladies' room – but everyone agreed that the toilets were badly in need of renovating. My mother was very much in favour of a new kitchen.

As it happened the whole idea was shelved when father put forward an older idea of my mother's to convert the large 'Buff's' room on the first floor to a small restaurant with an integral kitchen. Mister John thought it a splendid idea and said he would ask the architects to take another look at the pub but he promised that the toilets would be a first priority regardless of what happened to the upstairs room.

Father set off for home. In the time since he had arrived at the brewery a real pea-souper of a fog had settled on the town. It was one of those thick, yellow, sulphurous fogs that were common before the onset of smokeless zones. As he was about to get into his car he was approached by one of the office staff who asked if he could have a lift to Oldford. My father readily agreed but pointed out that the fog would make it a long and possibly hazardous journey. But the man was most grateful and explained that he was asthmatic and to be outside on a day like this – waiting for a bus for example – would be highly dangerous.

Before he got into the car he asked if my father would just hang on for a minute. He went into the office and returned immediately with a young fellow. Before my father had time to react it was explained that the newcomer, one of the office clerks, was the current West Riding cross country champion who also lived in Oldford and that he was prepared to run in front of father's car with a white handkerchief tucked into the back of his coat collar. It seemed a splendid idea and off they went.

The journey was uneventful and father reckoned he was home much quicker than he would have been if he had relied on his own navigation and the inadequate street lighting. The runner reached the bottom of the hill on the main road from Calderthorpe to Oldford and turned into the pub car park. Father followed him and parked. They got out of the car and to their amazement found that they had been followed by half a dozen other cars that had also turned into the car park. My father and his two colleagues stood amused as they watched the antics of the other drivers trying to extricate themselves from their self-made traffic jam. At least three of them gave up particularly as at that moment the pub lights were switched on for opening time.

Later that evening dad related the story to a few cronies, including Norman Dyson, who amused everyone with his tale of a foggy night in Calderthorpe some years ago. Not wanting the responsibility of finding his way all the way home he drove to the bus station and waited for what he thought was an Oldford bus to start its trip. He duly followed it for about three miles, dutifully waiting behind it at every stop.

One stop seemed to be much, much longer than the rest. He wondered if there was some mishap or other, so he got out of his car to investigate and found himself the object of considerable amusement and derision from the staff of the bus depot where the service had terminated that evening because of the adverse weather. The rest of his journey was long and uncomfortable and it was some time before he admitted the tale to anyone.

CHAPTER 6

....

OTHER LANDLORDS' TALES

"God I thank thee, that I am not as other men are,
extortioners, unjust, adulterers, or even as this publican."
THE GOSPEL ACCORDING TO ST LUKE

ON THEIR NIGHTS OFF LANDLORDS and landladies usually visit other pubs. I often asked my father why he didn't take my mother to the cinema. It seemed that a drink with their peers was the established practice and so it would remain. In fairness they often went off to the coast or the dales for a drive, taking the girls with them when they were on school holidays. Occasionally I would take my mother to the theatre in Calderthorpe or even Leeds and, on Saturdays father and I would scramble away after closing time to watch a game at one of the local football or rugby league clubs.

Come Wednesday however, rain or shine, mother and father would either walk across to the George to see Bert and Dot Cox and have returned the hospitality they had offered the night before, or take the car up to Bessie's on the top of Dogmoor.

Bessie's was an institution. She was the longest serving and oldest licensee in the West Riding of Yorkshire, or so she claimed and nobody had challenged her. She took over the pub in 1926 when her husband died after his car crashed through a fence and down a high banking during a blizzard. After 25 years in charge she refused a celebratory dinner by the Licensed Victuallers

Association on the grounds that her beloved Fred wasn't there to share it with her and then went on to hold her own party for regulars on the grounds that that was what Fred would have wanted her to do. 'Stuffy lot, the LVA,' she said afterwards. 'It would have been a dull party.'

More properly it was called the Dog and Partridge though folk for miles around only knew it as 'Bessie's'. Its original function was to serve the tiny hamlet of Snowberry but it had long been the haunt of walkers and was now dealing with the burgeoning car trade. It was a tiny pub with two small rooms served by a small bar in the parlour with a hatch to the vaults – a genuine vault where up to the 1920s casks of beer had been stored. The cellar was built by Fred after they moved there in 1919. Now Bessie worked the pub herself with the help of her son, Frank, who lived in the village.

Fred's modernisation had been simply to build the cellar, to allow drinkers more room in the vault, and to enlarge the tiny kitchen. It was in here that Bessie performed her miracles and her ham-and-egg meals were renowned throughout Yorkshire. On summer Sundays the expansive garden – the only thing about Bessie's that was large – would echo with the cries and games of children whilst their parents tucked into massive portions of home cured ham and free range eggs with chunks of home baked bread smothered in what was still called 'best butter' – a recall to wartime economies. The choice of pots of tea or Bessie's excellent ale was left to customers.

The bar closed at two o'clock on Sundays but food service continued until it opened again at seven. There was never any shortage of customers and Bessie with the help of 'young' Doris, just two years her junior, would keep them supplied with food whilst Frank managed the bar. What Bessie's lacked was some decent toilets, particularly for women. It was alright during the week when she had only her regulars to contend with but when the weekenders invaded the facilities were inadequate.

The gents were just about sufficient; two standups and a sitdown. But for the ladies things weren't so easy. There was just one compartment with an unusual, if not unique, double-seater toilet. It was OK for friends and relations but embarrassing if a lady was on her own and the queue was long. But despite these restrictions the crowds continued to come and Bessie continued to put off the job of building new toilets. Frank pleaded with her and had even gone to the trouble of obtaining planning permission for a small block behind the pub, but the old lads in her tap room, small 'c' conservative to a man, backed her up. 'They've nivver 'ad 'em afoore, so why should they 'ave 'em now?'

The crunch came one dark night when a young woman new to the pub asked where the toilets were. She was handed a torch and told how to find her way there. When installed she placed her handbag on what she thought was a bench alongside. Her task performed she reached for the bag only to find it had vanished. She returned to the pub somewhat distraught whereupon Frank, realising what had happened, said he would go and look for it. With a walking stick he hooked out the handbag from the depths of the second toilet, washed it off under the pump and returned it to the lady saying that he had been caught in a sudden shower. She didn't question the fact that Frank was still bone dry but gathered up the bag and her dumbstruck companion, muttered a perfunctory 'good night' and departed, never to return to discover the cosy comfort secrets of Bessie's outdoor double seater. Three weeks later work started on the new indoor toilets. Just for ladies!

🍺 🍺 🍺 🍺 🍺 🍺 🍺 🍺 🍺 🍺

Tommy Jones had a little pub, the Acorn, just outside the town in a quiet little valley known to all as 't'top nook'. It was not a busy pub and Tommy, a widower, managed to maintain a job as a journeyman plumber as well as run the pub. He was a pleasant enough sort of bloke and I always enjoyed a pint of his well-kept bitter from the Dawkins brewery up in the dales. Tommy had a little secret that I discovered one Friday evening when he asked Brian Dyson and me to 'stay behind for one'.

The pub soon emptied except for half a dozen of Tommy's mates and ourselves. We got drinks and settled down for what we expected to be an hour or so of pleasant conversation. But the rest had other ideas and out came the cards and, what seemed to me, considerable quantities of money. We had got ourselves into a regular card school and Tommy had assumed that we knew about it and wanted to play. My gambling went no further than a bob each way on the Grand National and penny nap after Christmas dinner. Brian was more adventurous but this was out of his league. We thanked Tommy who bought us another drink, finished it up and slid away into the night.

I thought no more about it and was discreet enough to keep quiet about Tommy's card school. Brian, I think, did the same. But someone else didn't. Colin Snapeson, a bit of a fly boy and well-known ladies man, who had been a member of the school in its early days had got into an affair with a local woman and used the card school as an excuse to his wife for his returning home in the early hours of most Saturday mornings. She accepted this for a while but eventually made up her mind to put a stop to it.

Came midnight on one Summer Friday and Mrs Snapeson rang the police to say that there was gambling and late drinking going on at the Acorn, then ringing off without giving her name. The police sergeant on duty realised that he had to do something about it. Normally he would have given Tommy a ring to say he was coming round but there was a relief inspector in charge who was a bit of a stickler. So off he went with a pair of constables and nicked Tommy and six others for drinking after time. The gambling was overlooked. Snapeson came home at 3 am saying he had been playing cards at the Acorn. He said nothing about the raid for the simple reason that he knew nothing about it.

On the following Tuesday the seven appeared at Oldford magistrates court where the customers were fined five pounds each. Tommy Jones was fined £25 and also given a severe warning as to his future conduct. Colin Snapeson was not, of course, prosecuted and Mrs Snapeson wanted to know the reason why not. Whether she found out isn't recorded but what is known is that the following day she kicked him out of the matrimonial home. And within a year she married Tommy Jones.

🐚 🐚 🐚 🐚 🐚 🐚 🐚 🐚 🐚 🐚

The 'Big' Crown in the centre of Oldford was a splendid old pub. It took its quantitative description because there was another Crown at the lower end of town. Both belonged to Harrison's brewery and both were late Victorian in construction. The 'Little' Crown was rather plain and only half the size of its more illustrious neighbour.

If Oldford had a gin palace then the 'Big' Crown was it, with masses of shining brass, polished mahogany and etched glass. A

The bar back was a delight

superb staircase was the centre piece of the pub with half a dozen high rooms leading off from the main bar. It was the haunt of businessmen and an ideal place to conduct deals. The dining room was well patronised for its reasonably priced and straight forward lunches: soup, cut off the joint with three veg. and a large helping of jam roly-poly or spotted dick and custard. Coffee included, all for three and sixpence.

David and Margaret Baines ran the pub. They were unusual in Oldford, where most licensees were either locals or at least from other parts of the West Riding, in being Londoners. It took my family a year or two to establish themselves and whilst my parents had been born only twenty miles away they were tainted by having lived in Lancashire. The Baines's had managed acceptance within six months by weight of personality. David was into most things in the town and he ran a lively tap room and Margaret's control of the dining room made her an immediate favourite with the commercials and professionals. The 'Big' Crown had a lot going for it.

The bar back was a delight with mirrors and broad shelving hosting antique glassware and some ornate porcelain spirit caskets complete with spigots which David decided to bring back into use. It meant the inconvenience of using measures instead of optics but he thought they added to the style of the pub. There was a pink container for rum, a gold one for whisky and two white ones for gin and he was very proud of them. Each time they were empty David would scald them clean and leave them full of cold water for an hour or so. He would then empty them and fill up with about eight bottles of the appropriate spirit.

One Tuesday evening David went off with my father, Bert Cox and a few other licensees to a reception held by a wine company at a hotel high up the valley. It was a men-only do and they were not expected back until late. Taxis had been laid on. Tuesday was a quiet evening and I had taken a walk around town with Bernard Lynn, one of our regulars, captain of the local cricket team and an interesting all round bloke. Mother was in charge at the Coach and Four and Margaret was in charge at the 'Big' Crown, which was our first stop. I had a 'thing' about Margaret and she knew it because she always made a fuss, occasionally embarrassing me.

We expected the pub to be reasonably quiet but it was buzzing and Margaret and one barmaid were run off their feet. It seemed that just after David had left, most of the town hall staff had come in following a union meeting at which they had presented a tankard to a very popular branch secretary who was on the move. There had also been a pay rise after prolonged negotiations and they all had pockets full of back pay. The drink flowed free.

I offered to help for half an hour to keep the wolves at bay. Shorts seemed to be the order with the chaps on whisky and the women on gin. I was rewarded with a pint of bitter and a peck on the cheek from Margaret that made me feel great. After another drink Bernard and I left them to their own rather noisy devices and sought more placid climes.

It was some weeks later before I visited the 'Big' Crown again and Margaret took me on one side making me feel rather special.

'Do you remember the last time you were in here, with that cricketer bloke, when you helped behind the bar?' Obviously I did. 'Did you serve a lot of gin?' she asked.

I told her I did, and a lot of whisky.

'Never mind the whisky,' said Margaret, 'it was the gin. David had cleaned out one of the caskets and left it full of water. I assumed it was full of gin and put it back on the shelf. All night long we were serving from the two containers, sometimes they got gin, sometimes water. And nobody complained so they must have had a skinful.'

David joined us and we laughed about it. For the moment at least we were the only ones who knew what had happened. Later it became an open secret amongst friends and at parties or on the occasional after hours foray some wag would ask David or Margaret for 'a water and tonic please'.

The landlord of the Volunteer on the new estate was a former regular in the Royal Air Force called George Poole. What rank he had held was something he kept to himself, he was probably a corporal and there was nothing wrong in that – the folk who lived on the estate with their £2,000 mortgages, wouldn't have given a fig if he'd been an Air Vice Marshal. But he liked to maintain a certain presence. He was always smart with collar and tie from opening time to closing time, and he spoke in plummy tones, so they called him 'Winco' after some wag suggested that he must have been a Wing Commander at least. He accepted it as nothing less than he deserved. His wife Lucy had a similar disposition and enjoyed lauding it over other landlord's wives at LVA ladies' do's where she invariably took the chair. Norman had a party piece in which he used to call them the Right Honourable Wing Commander Sir George Poole DFC and bar, JP, MP, SOD, and Lady Poole. For my part, I liked them both.

Winco ran the tightest ship in Oldford if you could excuse that phrase for a former airman. He never allowed late drinking even for other licensees who generally regarded one another as fair game so long as it wasn't overdone. His plaintive 'Sorry, sir, towels are up' greeted many a thirsty customer at 31 minutes past ten when in every other pub in town the final pints were still being pulled. But he cleared his lines, washed the glasses, swept the floor and emptied the ashtrays every night before retiring; he kept excellent ale, called every male customer 'Sir' and every woman 'Madam'. He ran the place with the discipline one expected of a former regular serviceman and there was never any trouble. The Volunteer was an appropriately named pub for Winco although Norman occasionally called it 'the Barracks'.

However well he kept his beer it wasn't for some reason good enough for Winco. He usually drank bottled Guinness or pink gins. If you asked him to join you in a pint he would refuse and all suggestions that a man who managed to keep the best pint of Harrison's bitter in the area ought to drink his own product were met with a: 'Thank you, sir, I'm sure it's very good but I'll stick to my own poison.'

When pressed the most he would reveal was that his father had been 'overly fond of Harrison's bitter'. However it had not rubbed off on him. The strange thing was that when he occasionally visited pubs belonging to a different brewery he had been seen to drink a pint of draught bitter.

Norman was intrigued. Like me he was very fond of Winco not just because of his precise form of speech which amused us but because he was generous to all around, supported charities and had a genuine love of his fellow men. Norman believed there was a bohemian figure trying to escape from Winco's rather staid frame.

Lucy Poole had a son from a previous marriage living in Australia. She hadn't seen him since he emigrated and he now had a family of three. The son invited her to go out for a visit and she dearly wanted to go. Winco reluctantly agreed and she took the boat from Tilbury and was away for three months. It was during this period that Norman struck.

With collar and tie from opening time to closing time

He arranged an after hours party at David Baines's pub, the 'Big' Crown, claiming it was thirty years since he drank his first pint and that this was the pub he drank it in. All the usual crowd were invited – 'the glitterati of Oldford' as Norman put it – and Margaret Baines laid on a splendid buffet. By midnight the party was in full swing and amongst the latecomers was Winco. I must say I was surprised but Norman had insisted that he take a night off to enjoy himself particularly as Lucy was on the other side of the world.

Norman plied him with pink gins but no amount of persuasion would tempt him to a pint of Harrison's. 'It's almost as good as yours,' we told him. But he merely responded that he was sure it was and initially his only concession to the occasion was to drop the 'Sir' and 'Madam' and address people personally. Norman got 'Norman' and David got 'David', but Margaret was 'Mrs Baines' and I was 'Young Mister Lowe'. However, as the night progressed, so Winco's defences started to slip.

The first indication was when he joined in the singing to Ronnie Taylor's piano medley. Then he sang one of his own in a most acceptable baritone. He admitted to having 'done a bit' (of singing presumably) when he was younger. The pink gins went down and Norman and Winco got into an intimate conversation which produced plenty of laughter. It was, as Winco said in his own pub a week or so later: 'A night to remember, sir, we ought to do it again sometime.'

Norman was fit to bust when I went down the cellar with him the following Saturday morning to do our usual pipe cleaning exercise. 'I've found out why Winco won't drink Harrison's beer.' It seemed that the huddle the two of them had been in at the party had been confession time for Winco brought about by an excess of pink gins.

His father, another George Poole, had worked at Harrison's brewery from the turn of the century and had risen to become a shift brewer. As Winco often said he was 'overly fond' of the product and he was a dedicated workman. He died in 1920 in somewhat mysterious circumstances when George Poole junior was only 13 years old. The newspapers gave the outcome of an inquest as 'death by misadventure' and talk was of an industrial accident.

Winco knew the real story. His father had been on a trip to the coast with the brewery draymen and they had consumed quite a lot. 'Stopped twice for a pee between Malton and Norton' as one wag put it. (Only the River Derwent separates the two towns!) The charabanc dropped the men off at the brewery in Calderthorpe and, despite his condition, Mister Poole senior went to check on his brews. The night-watchman let him in and assumed that he had left shortly afterwards. It was the following morning when his body was found in the number one fermenting vessel. The facts were hushed up and the Harrison family carried enough clout in the town to keep it that way. Mrs Poole was given a generous pension and it was only in her late years that she told young George the full tale.

Norman swore me to secrecy and we agreed that in similar circumstances we would be hardly likely to drink the beer. Many years later Norman phoned me to tell me that Winco had died out in Australia where he and Lucy had retired to. We reminisced for a while and Norman said that he would now be reunited with his father and they could drink a pint of nectar together.

🍺 🍺 🍺 🍺 🍺 🍺 🍺 🍺 🍺 🍺

The Dog and Duck was at the other end of the town centre to the Coach and Four. It was not a pub I frequented and my parents kept their visits down to a minimum. The main reason was the landlord, Ronnie Clitheroe, a self-opinionated man who had never been wrong in his life.

The landlady, Joyce, was a pleasant girl, very loyal to her husband but who gave the impression that given half a chance she would slip the lead and go her own way. My mother liked her a lot and often said she would like to spend more time with her but it meant putting up with 'that awful Ronnie'.

Ronnie not only had strong views on most matters but he was also a bigot, a racist and very full of his own importance. At least that was how I saw him and so, I gathered, did most other folk. Norman's view was that the pub scene in Oldford would be a lot better if the Dog and Duck got a new landlord. He occasionally said this to Ronnie Clitheroe in his best 'I don't suffer fools gladly' manner only to receive a smiling reply of 'you're always kidding me, Norman.' Clitheroe actually thought he was popular.

The Clitheroes were in their fifties and both were in their second marriages. Joyce had a daughter, Jane, who was married to Trevor Berryman, a likeable bloke who drove a bus and shared most folks' view on his father in law. But they had a young family and at weekends Trevor worked on the bar at the Dog and Duck to eke out his regular wage.

Ronnie and Joyce decided to take an autumn holiday in Blackpool. It was for a week during the illuminations and several other licensee couples were going along. The pub's bar-cellarman, a simple but honest chap called Dick Dixon took charge of the Dog and Duck.

On the Monday evening of the holiday, around eight o' clock in the evening, the phone rang. Dick answered it to find Ronnie enquiring how things were at the Dog. He was told all was in order and things, as on most Mondays, were pretty slack.

'Are there many in the tap room?' asked Ronnie.

'Six or seven,' said Dick.

'Well get them a drink on me,' came the response from a land-lord who along with his other faults was not noted for his generosity. Dick told the bemused tap room crowd that Ronnie must be enjoying his holiday.

Two days later at about the same time the phone went again and a similar conversation ensued. This time there were a dozen or so in the tap room and those who had enjoyed the hospitality previously were more than surprised. The Clitheroes must be having a great week in Blackpool.

When the same thing happened on Friday the twenty recipients of Ronnie Clitheroe's bounty included one or two who had heard of the phenomena and had decided to get in on the act. One of them was Trevor Berryman who found the whole business highly amusing.

Just after nine o' clock the phone went again and Ronnie Clitheroe was there again asking after the health of the pub. Dick was a bit confused but said everything was OK and the lads in the tap room were very appreciative of the drinks Ronnie had sent in for them.

There was an explosion from the Blackpool end of the line.

'WHAT DRINKS?' shouted Ronnie.

'The ones you told me to get in for the lads in the tap room when you rang earlier. And on Monday and Wednesday,' cowered Dick.

The rest of the conversation was difficult to follow. Dick told the tap room crowd who found it very funny, particularly the landlord's son-in-law. Dick said that Ronnie had told him that the cost of the drinks would come out of his wages, and he responded that if it did then he would be leaving. The regulars said they would pay for their drinks if the miserable beggar tried that one on.

Ronnie was back before ten o' clock the following morning trailed by an unhappy Joyce. There was an almighty row during which Dick told him what to do with his job and the story spread around Oldford like wildfire. Ronnie had been conned and most folk thought it wasn't before time.

Although I had my suspicions it was two years before I learned the truth that Trevor Berryman had been one of the blokes behind the dupe. He had nipped out to a phone box next to the pub and imitated Ronnie's rather snivelling voice. I also had an idea that Norman Dyson had something to do with it but he would never admit it, merely winking and saying: 'It couldn't happen to a nicer fellow.'

The annual dinner and ball of the Oldford and District Licensed Victuallers' Association was a posh do. It was held in the Royal George, a large residential hotel high above the town with an imposing facade and splendid views across the town and the valley.

Everybody who fancied themselves in Oldford went to the LVA dinner. The Mayor was the chief guest although whoever was the President of the Licensed Victuallers' Defence League of England and Wales liked to think that he was. And, of course, the local LVA President was a pretty important figure too. At least he thought so. The whole affair was full of swells and folk thinking they were swells.

I felt rather down market amongst the town's hierarchy on the first occasion that my father invited me. 'You can bring a guest if you like,' he said with a twinkle. This was no doubt a reference to the fact that I didn't have a steady girl friend. I told him I would do just that.

My father held no office in the LVA but he had decided that as the dinner was being held in the week between his and my mother's birthday he would make a party of it. He booked a table for twenty, invited most of his closer friends from the town along with his two brothers and their wives and my cousin Colin and his wife.

'Tell your friend to wear a long dress,' said my mother. 'That'll be interesting,' I said. 'I wonder what Bernard Lynn will look like in a dress?'

In fact I had decided to take Liz Harman, a fellow teacher at my school in Leeds. I owed her one for the several times she had invited me to her home for a meal and occasionally a bed for the night when we had to stay late for parents' evenings, staff do's and the like. Mother was delighted to put her up for the night and my two sisters were inventing all sorts of romantic tales about us. She was good company and could hold her own in Oldford. I admired her independent spirit.

The old man had made up his mind that we would have a good night out but he reckoned without the top table. The evening was, however, saved by the Mayor.

Dad and Norman explained the form beforehand. We would have a few drinks at the pub – 'to get a glow on' according to Norman – and then taxi it up to the Royal George where one of the whisky suppliers was laying on a reception. 'Don't drink their whisky,' warned Norman, 'it's all their old rubbish they want to off load.'

There was a long top table for the nobs and the rest of the room was filled with circular tables for parties from the various pubs. Ours was on the outside, which according to Norman was strategic: 'We can nip out to the bar or the toilet without disturbing anyone and we can keep an eye on the rest of the mob.'

The preliminaries went according to plan if seeing and be seen was the plan. Landlords' wives certainly know how to put on the style and a good few hundred quids' worth of haute couture was on display that night. Everybody seemed to have the same idea

"I wonder what Bernard Lynn will look like in a dress?"

too. They all arrived with a glow on and few were touching the whisky.

Councillor Alfie Hetherington was the Mayor of Oldford that year. He was one of our regulars and he upset the top brass by spending most of the reception talking to the party from the Coach and Four. Eventually it was time for dinner and we moved to our table.

On my right was Liz and on my left was Norman who was keeping the company amused with his potted biographies of the folk on the top table.

....

'There goes Winco in his year of office as President of the Oldford LVA. I bet he puts letters after his name; something like POLVA – sounds like a Polish drink.

'And what a man to have as treasurer,' he went on. 'Ronnie Clitheroe is not only the most miserable landlord in Oldford, he's also the meanest. I bet the Mayor had to pay for his own drinks.' Clitheroe's unpopularity was well known.

'But if you think he's tight then look who's next to Alfie Hetherington.' Norman was working his way along the table. 'It's Clarence Thornton from the Rock in Calderthorpe, he must be the regional LVA chairman or some such nonsense. He bites two bob pieces to see if they're genuine and runs the only pub in Yorkshire that sells half pork pies.'

We were enjoying ourselves. However the meal was pretty good if a bit pretentiously described. Liz summed it up and endeared herself to my family: 'If we're going to get peas with our duck why do they have to call them "Les Petits Pois Parisienne"? I bet the nearest they've been to Paris is Lincolnshire.'

So far so good. But a careful perusal of the menu ought to have warned us. There were three toasts, apart from the Queen, two of them with one response and the other with two; seven speeches in all. There was a short break after the meal and Norman started a sweep on the time the speeches would finish. 'Be lucky if we're home before the light,' he quipped.

The speeches started. A toast to the Oldford LVA from the National President was responded to by Winco and the local secretary, a dull-as-dust solicitor with the sense of humour of a politician who had just lost his seat. They took the best part of an hour.

Then there was a toast to the trade. David Baines made a good stab at both being funny and being brief. He was a Londoner who ran the 'Big' Crown, a popular guy and a friend of ours. The bloke who followed him did not match his intentions. Not only was Mister Simpson Borrowdale, Chairman of Borrowdale Breweries, long-winded and boring he was incoherent and pretty drunk as well. Half way through his speech he forgot where he was and launched into a tirade against the government for raising the tax on spirits in the last budget some six months before. 'Must have been at the cheap whisky,' said Norman.

The final toast to Our Guests raised our spirits a little. The proposer was Winco again, and the response would be from Alfie – the Mayor. Liz nudged me and said that she hoped someone would wake the Mayor up in time to make his speech. Alfie certainly looked asleep but I suspected he was having us on.

Winco, sadly, hadn't taken his cue and wound his patient way through his prepared speech of around 20 minutes. Open yawning was the order of the evening. Conversations were taking place quite openly all around the room and there was a large crowd in the bar ignoring the formalities and waiting for the dancing. Our table, however, remained loyal to Alfie and he in turn was loyal to us.

He stood up, faced the audience and said: 'It's my job to thank the LVA on behalf of the guests for our meal. It's been grand.' And he sat down to tumultuous cheers. The dancing started and as I had won the sweep I had to buy the next round.

THE BREWER'S TALE

"Oh I'm the man, the very fat man,
that waters the workers' beer."
PADDY RYAN

MY FATHER HAD ONLY MET JOHN HARRISON, the managing director of the brewery, on a couple of occasions, one being when he and my mother were interviewed for the job as tenants of the Coach and Four. The other was when he was called in to discuss alterations to the pub. If asked what he thought about the man who was regarded as 'running the brewery' he would have said that he seemed an amiable sort of bloke who wouldn't do you a bad turn but who, nevertheless, had the best interests of the shareholders – that is, mainly himself and his family – in mind.

Harrison's was very much a family brewery and somewhat paternalistic in its make-up and philosophy. The Harrison family involvement in the business – and John Harrison was the nephew of the great grandson of Spencer Harrison who founded the firm in 1849 – was mirrored by its workforce. The present head brewer had followed his father into the job; three of the coopers were from one family; and one of the draymen was a fourth generation to be employed at Harrison's. Some of the pub tenants went back a long way with Bessie at the Dog and Partridge in Snowberry holding the record, having taken over from her husband in 1926 after he had held the licence for seven years.

John Harrison, as is the way of these things, being the oldest son had moved into the managing director's seat when his uncle died just after the war. 'Master John' had served with distinction as a major in the Royal Engineers and received the Military Cross for his part in the Arnhem landings. He was honest and fair to his workers and they regarded him with similar respect. Less could be said of Peter Harrison, who called himself 'Sales Director', but was in reality a salesman to the free trade. He was haughty and apt to get folks' backs up but, fortunately, was rarely seen around the tied houses.

The area managers, five of them, looked after the tied trade. In fact, if truth were known, apart from producing the essential product, they ran the brewery. Jack Thornton was our area manager, a likeable man loyal both to the firm and to the tenants he served. Others had lesser reputations but Jack could always find plenty of advertising material, beer mats and the like, and there were always a few pounds available for minor decorations. But he was a hard man to negotiate with and father and he had some heated discussions on the issue of a major refurbishment to the Coach and Four.

It was during this period that my father rang the brewery to raise a query with Jack Thornton. A voice said 'Harrison's Brewery'.

Father asked for Mister Thornton to be told that he was out for the moment but expected back within the hour.

'Who's that?' came the enquiry from the brewery end of the line.

'It's Alex Lowe from the Coach and Four in Oldford.'

'Oh, hello Mister Lowe, it's John Harrison here, I'll get Mister Thornton to phone you when he returns.'

The old man was amused and asked if Mister Harrison did telephone duty regularly. 'Well, we all have to muck in, don't you know,' he responded.

About an hour later Jack Thornton rang back and father and he settled their bit of business. Father then asked: 'By the way, Jack, how long has Master John been your telephone operator?'

Jack laughed. 'Oh we don't mind him doing that or even signing letters and cheques so long as we can keep him away from the goods inward book.'

"Well we all have to muck in, don't you know"

Father had an arrangement with the draymen. They delivered the bulk of his order on a Tuesday morning – usually six hogsheads of bitter, four of Best and three barrels of mild – and then what was known as a slip order on Friday afternoon. The amount of this would vary according to how sales had gone during the week and what might be expected during the weekend. The brewery frowned upon this system expecting licensees to take in sufficient stocks on their regular weekly delivery and only have slip orders if absolutely necessary. But because the Coach and Four sold a lot of beer a blind eye was turned.

The Friday drop was the last of the week for the three draymen and this suited them for they all lived in Oldford and by the time they had lowered the beer into the cellar and parked up the dray in a corner of the car park it was five o'clock and the pub was open. And the first drink was always on the landlord. The three of them were darts daft and would monopolise the board for a couple of hours when, suitably replete, they would wander home to dried up dinners and frigid wives. But they spent quite a lot and father indulged them – it did no harm to keep well in with the draymen.

One evening they were well oiled by seven o'clock, the driver, Harold Royston, in particular. He could hardly stand but it was an important game and he was involved in it. He needed double top to win and his first dart missed the board and ricocheted off the overhead lampshade. The second one nearly speared an old codger quietly enjoying a pint in the corner. Harold was determined to make it with his last dart but on taking aim fell flat on his face.

They picked him up and he attempted once more to take aim, this time staggering across the room.

'Gimmeabrush,' he growled.

'What?' asked his mates.

'A brush,' said Harold.

There was a large sweeping brush alongside the fireplace and it was passed to him. By this time the entire tap room was silent and watching Harold's performance with fascination. He turned the brush upside down and propped the head against his chest, wedging the end of the handle at an angle of 45 degrees to support him. When he was properly secure he aimed, threw and scored a double top. And then fell flat on his face.

Jack Wilkinson was another drayman who whilst he didn't deliver to us was a regular at the Coach and Four. He offered to take me one Saturday morning to the brewery maltings just outside Skipton. He and his mate, Billy Bickerdyke, picked me up at the pub at seven o'clock and off we went, stopping at one of the brewery's pubs near Keighley for some breakfast. Billy was a quiet type and whilst Jack and I tucked into bacon and eggs and a large pot of tea he, despite the early hour, emptied a couple of pint bottles of pale ale.

At the maltings I was given the full treatment by the manager who was pleased to see someone from one of the pubs showing an interest in his work. There was a racked barrel of bitter and we were invited to have a drink. Jack and I had a couple of halves and Billy, at a conservative guess, had three pints. But it might have been four, or even five. On the way back we stopped at a favourite pub of mine high over the valley where we were treated by the landlord – halves for Jack and me, a pint for Billy, and then he had another. The next stop was at the brewery to unload the malt and to park up the dray. Then we had another drink in the staff bar with Billy putting it away with some energy. Jack suggested going to see the local soccer club, Calderthorpe Town, a middling Third Division North side with its ground less than a mile from the brewery. 'Why not?' we said.

There was an acceptable transport café nearby much used by Harrison's draymen and we called there for pies, peas and chips and pint mugs of tea. This was a novelty for Billy who by that time had drunk about a dozen pints of beer. He had also achieved the unique feat of not having been to the toilet since we started out about seven hours earlier. And it was the tea that did for him. From that moment on he was up and down like a yoyo. He hardly saw any of the game and the suggestion at half time that we have a cup of tea was met with an icy stare and a grunted 'no'.

My father and mother were preparing for the 'visit and inter-view'. This was one of managing director John Harrison's inno-vations. The brewery owned about 150 pubs, about half tenanted and half managed, and the five area managers kept an eye on around 30 each. The system worked well but Mister Harrison believed, so he said, in 'progressive and modern management' and two years ago had announced his intention of visiting each of the tied houses annually. The plan was for him, one or two of the other directors and the appropriate area manager to arrive unexpectedly, have a look around the pub and then conduct what became known as 'the interview'. The whole affair was anything but unexpected because the area managers usually warned the licensees who awaited the visit with varying degrees of trepidation.

John Harrison's ideas on management were a joke. No one quite understood what 'progressive and modern management' meant, particularly as the company offices still had high stools and sloping desks and had only recently had electric lighting installed. The brewery was Victorian and so were the systems. The pubs were kept in good condition and this made the company ripe for take-over. But Mister Harrison went on these visits in the firm belief that he was doing something innovative.

Jack Thornton warned my father that Master John would be with us around eleven-thirty on the Wednesday morning just before Easter. Came the day and Norman and I had given the cellar a thorough going-over although Norman regarded this as a slur on his cellar-keeping abilities. 'I keep the place in perfect order,' he told the old man, 'And I don't mind if the Queen comes to inspect it never mind a jumped-up popinjay of a brewery direc-tor!' We all took Norman with a pinch of salt and nevertheless, with my help, he did a good job of preparing the cellar. 'We'll call it a spring clean,' my father suggested and that seemed to satisfy Norman.

Mother was supervising the cleaners who were taking the same attitude as Norman but she had them on a tight rein. Vera was giving the glass stock an extra polish. Father in his usual placid way was observing all this activity and making the point that when John Harrison does his visits then he must know that an extra effort has been put in. 'If he wants to catch us out he ought to just appear in the middle of a busy evening session.' But John Harrison wasn't like that; he was shy and withdrawn and the idea of walking into any of his pubs on his own was not his way.

Why, I asked myself, should father worry?

'Try and look casual,' was his advice as the witching hour approached.

I wondered what Mister Harrison would make of our spotless and obviously overstaffed pub?

A large limousine drew up outside and Mister Harrison, his brother Peter and the company secretary got out of it and came in to the pub. Father was called from upstairs where he was determined to be when the party arrived. Jack Thornton came in from his own car in the car park where he had been hiding for the last quarter of an hour, or so he thought. Mother put on a great show of surprise and the old man came down the stairs in his shirt sleeves looking every bit the harassed and overworked landlord. I think the directors were impressed.

Father took them on a conducted tour of the pub. First the public rooms and then what Peter Harrison, who could be a pompous ass, called 'the usual offices'. He meant the toilets. We were fortunate that the toilets at the Coach and Four did not seem to attract the usual spate of graffiti. It took someone like Peter to find a piece behind the door of one of the cubicles in the ladies of all places. It said: 'Flush twice – it's uphill to the brewery.' He was not amused but the rest of the party seemed unconcerned and the incident passed. Then it was the turn of the cellar.

Father had the devil's own job to keep Norman out of the way. He knew that the slightest word of criticism would lead to an almighty row. We learned afterwards that there was only the highest praise for the state of the cellar but, as the company secretary – who liked his ale – said: 'It's the taste that counts, perhaps Mister Lowe we could sample a drop of your beer?' There was ready agreement and the party went upstairs. Father drew off half a dozen glasses of Best and there were certainly no complaints, although Peter Harrison made a fool of himself by holding his glass to the light and trying to find fault with the clarity. 'The only thing he'll see,' whispered Norman, 'is good honest beer – cheeky bugger.'

And so, after a quick look at the office and the private quarters, to 'the interview'. Mother had laid on a 'spontaneous' buffet lunch in the snug and the glasses were refilled before she and father joined the brewery party. It lasted about twenty minutes, most of which was said to be spent in eating. Out they trooped and the big smile on Jack Thornton's face told everything. Peter Harrison had asked a couple of daft questions but it was what his brother thought that mattered and he seemed well satisfied. They had another drink and prepared to leave.

Just as John Harrison reached the front door he turned and called out to my father: 'A moment please, Mister Lowe.' The old man went over. 'By the way, I'm certain that your house is always in good order and I'm sure if I came in here at any time I would be happy with what I found. But next time we come and Mister Thornton lets you know in advance, it would be better not to ring the day on the calendar and mark the work rota so obviously displayed in your office with the words: BREWERY VISIT! Good afternoon, Mister Lowe.'

🍺 🍺 🍺 🍺 🍺 🍺 🍺 🍺 🍺 🍺

The main road from Oldford to Calderthorpe wound steeply up Bishop's Mound and then dropped over into the next valley where the dark satanic mills of the larger town held prominence. Harrison's brewery was in the centre of town and like most of the larger breweries in the West Riding retained its stables and a number of dray horses.

At its steepest parts, and on the bends, the road was still cobbled although few horses used it these days. Except for those driven by Bert Walls. It was Harrison's practice to use their half dozen dray horses as much as possible. During the summer they were entered into the various shows in the county and occasionally shown off at other functions. But their real purpose, as John Harrison often said, was to deliver beer. He was once quoted in the Morning Advertiser as saying: 'When a motor dray is stopped at traffic lights it is still burning petrol. When a horse-drawn dray stops the animals are resting.' 'It's the first time that paper's ever had owt useful to say,' said a local landlord, and its tekken a Yorkshireman to say it.'

Horse drawn drays were mainly confined to the pubs in the centre of Calderthorpe. This was economic and it kept the brewery name in front of people in that town where Harrison's competed with two other similar sized firms. But occasionally they delivered to some of the smaller towns within striking distance of the brewery and Oldford was one of these.

By taking the long and gradual downhill drag out to the south of Calderthorpe a dray could turn on to the valley road with a leisurely trot into Oldford. Returning was easy enough because there was no weight of beer to carry, only empty casks. But this route was not for Bert Walls.

He had been with Harrison's White Rose Brewery for thirty years taking over as head horseman twelve years ago when his father had retired from the post. He was what is known as a 'character'. Which meant he had a sense of humour when it suited him but he could be a martinet at other times. Bert was as flexible as an electric light switch.

Most landlords liked him and welcomed the arrival of the horses. Despite Master John's view of the economic nature of the horses – another of his quotes in the Morning Advertiser was 'hay and bran's a lot cheaper than petrol and oil' – there was a public relations factor that could not easily be quantified. Bert Walls understood this and that was why if he had to take a dray to Oldford he took it down, and up, the main road.

Bert wasn't bothered about the weather either, possibly drawing the line at snow when he would protect his charges and not allow them out of the stables even for town deliveries. But rain wouldn't put him off and he regarded a wet slippery road down to Oldford as a challenge. He would keep a tight rein on the two horses and expect his assistant to operate the hand brake to his unspoken wishes. Woe betide the lad if he failed to apply it on a bend or released it too quickly. The side of Bert Walls without a sense of humour came through very sharply then. On the other hand the man who knitted in with his thoughts would receive the highest praise for a job well done.

Returning to the brewery also needed skill but this came mainly from Bert who would coax the horses with promises of 'lovely 'arrison's ale and lots of 'ay' for them if they kept up the pace. There were even parts of the hill where he would trot them with his loving, cajoling, persuasive voice always there to urge them on.

'He talks to them horses,' said one of his fellow horsemen to my father one morning during a delivery.

'You all do,' said my father.

'Ah, yes,' said the man, 'but they bloody well understand him.'

There was a view, particularly among the motor draymen at the brewery that Bert Walls would meet his Waterloo on the way down from Calderthorpe to Oldford one cold, wet, misty morning. It was more of a hope than a view in the minds of some of them. Horsemen and motormen had the same sort of relationship as detectives and uniformed policemen, professional and amateur cricketers. But it was not to be.

A pint of Best for Spencer

113

He met it on the way up on a warm, dry, bright afternoon.

Bert had two particular favourites amongst the horses. They were oldest of his charges, Spencer and Bessie, named after the founder of the brewery and his wife. They were approaching retirement and Bert continually regaled them with tales of the lovely fields out at Skipton where dray horses spent the autumn of their lives. Spencer, in particular, enjoyed his beer and the gallon a day official ration was never enough for him. At most drops Bert would persuade the landlord to pull a pint of Best for Spencer. And, as if he knew retirement was due, the horse was thickening around the belly and increasing the amount he drank. On the day in question Spencer was thought to have had around five pints before starting the uphill trip back to the brewery.

It was early afternoon on a beautiful spring day and the sooner Bert got back to the brewery the sooner he could get home to his other love – breeding homing pigeons. According to the assistant horseman he was racing the drays a bit whilst still keeping to the traditional walk and trot pattern. There was no sign of any discomfort from Spencer when suddenly he seized up and stopped dead, literally, for he had suffered a fatal heart attack and the hill was just that bit too much for him. Bessie, taken by surprise, continued on her way and dragged the dray around in a half circle and on to its two offside wheels. Bert tried to draw in the reins but as Spencer's knees buckled and Bessie continued to pull her way forward, two ton of horse became too much for him and he fell off the dray to the ground with an almighty thump.

His fellow horseman managed the impossible and contained Bessie before the dray tipped over. For Bert though it was too late. His injuries were superficial, merely some cuts and a few bruises, but the psychological damage it did to him was enormous. 'It was his pride that got dented worse,' said his mate. 'He couldn't believe that after 30 years of demanding everything from the horses that not only would one of them die on him but that another was strong enough to dump him off the dray.'

Bert took a week off work and would willingly have never returned to the brewery, given half a chance. But he was still under 50 and retirement was not a possibility. It was the thought of returning to the smirks and jokes of the motormen that he could not face up to. But it had to be done. No one blamed him for the death of Spencer although he thought everybody did. What most people felt was that Albert had overdone it and the bruises were punishment enough and a warning to tone down his demanding, sergeant major attitude.

His return was at his usual starting time of five o'clock in the stables before most other folk were awake. It gave him the chance to put a couple of hours of hard work behind him polishing brasses and cleaning the harnesses before he had to face what he thought were his persecutors. Apart from the odd snigger kept well away from Bert it was no different that Monday morning to any other at Harrison's brewery. John Harrison had done his job well with the workforce. Now he had to do it with Bert.

It was simple enough. In future deliveries to Oldford would be by the long route, the main road was out of bounds. And, although no one ever so much as suggested it to him, Bert Walls took the decision himself never to deliver to Oldford again.

🍺 🍺 🍺 🍺 🍺 🍺 🍺 🍺 🍺

Looking after beer is a long and tender process. Unlike the modern day keg beers and lagers, traditional ales require care. You cannot have the casks dropped into the cellar and start serving from them immediately. The beer needs to settle and it needs a period of conditioning depending on how long it had been at the brewery in casks. Cleanliness in the cellar and in the bars is essential; temperatures have to be right and bar staff need to know how to pull a pint. If, after all this, the beer is not satisfactory then it is the brewery's fault.

That brief resumé, summed up my father's view and, more importantly at the Coach and Four at Oldford, that of Norman Dyson, bar cellarman extraordinaire.

'I'm not suggesting Harrison's get it wrong all that often,' said Norman one Saturday morning as we went through our usual business of cleaning the pumps and lines and making sure the beers were properly attended to. 'Take this barrel of mild. We've had a poor week on mild and it's probably just about past its best.

I've just dipped it and there's about 20 pints left which should go this lunchtime, otherwise I would suggest to your old man that we dump it. We certainly couldn't blame the brewery.

'On the other hand, a few weeks ago we had some bitter that wouldn't settle. Every one I pulled off was cloudy and I began to wonder if it was me doing something wrong. So I phoned 'Winco' at the Volunteer who probably keeps the best pint of Harrison's in Oldford.'

'After you,' I interrupted.

'After me,' he confirmed. 'And he was having the same trouble. Layering he called it; sometimes the beer was as clear as crystal and the next pint was cloudy.'

My father had phoned whom he called the 'brewery technical bloke' – in fact one of the young apprentice brewers – who came along and tried all sorts of methods to clear the beer. Finings, the usual way of doing it was showing no results and other methods such as a bottle of tonic water – a strictly illegal practice yet one advised by many breweries – followed by a good stir with the dip stick did no good either. Purists such as Norman would have winced at what happened. In the end he agreed to have the beer replaced.

Of course the weather could affect the beer. Thunderstorms had been known to have a disastrous effect, causing beer to turn cloudy and making it taste sour. The cellar at the Coach and Four was deep and well insulated. It was not artificially cooled but retained a fairly constant temperature of around 55 degrees Fahrenheit which was just right for cask beer. In winter my father would sometimes use an electric heater to hold the temperature.

It was a hot summer and lots of licensees were complaining about the condition of their beers. The Coach seemed to miss the worst with only a couple of barrels being returned. It was a job draymen hated as you can imagine; a full hogshead (54 gallons) weighs nearly three hundredweight – the same as three sacks of coal – and they had to manhandle them out of the cellar, often a lift of several feet, and then on to the dray.

An almost full hogshead was to be sent back to the brewery and a special dray had been sent out to do the job and presumably several similar ones in the area. The draymen were not our regulars who knew the layout of the cellar and the intricacies of the drop.

Using ropes with one man at the top and the other in the cellar they were taking the barrel up bit by bit when a rope slipped and the barrel tumbled to the cellar floor taking the drayman with it.

He was not as badly hurt as first imagined but the ambulance rushed him to Calderthorpe General along with his anxious mate and accompanied by my father. Two broken toes and some bruising to his legs along with a certain amount of shock for both workers was the result. Father came home by taxi to survey the damage to his cellar.

The wayward barrel had knocked over a tower of bottle crates and gone on to strike a row of racked barrels on a free standing stillage. Apart from a few broken bottles and the need to allow the barrels in use to settle down and clear again there was no other damage. Of course the barrel that caused all the trouble was still there and it would have to wait a few days before it could be removed.

The injured drayman was kept in hospital for a few days and his mate was back on the job straight away. The brewery got our regular draymen to lift the offending barrel on their next regular drop and replaced the broken bottles.

The following weekend relatives from South Yorkshire were visiting. They were a mining family and used to living with industrial accidents and their consequences. They were talking about a recent roof fall at their local pit and how lucky the colliers had been to get out. 'Miners,' said my father disparagingly, 'they don't know what danger means. It's in the pub business where all the big risks are.'

CHAPTER 8

....

THE POLICEMAN'S TALE

"It was the English who made hours for drinking."
GRAHAM GREENE

MY FATHER DECIDED TO HAVE a burglar alarm fitted. A number of pubs, mainly rural ones admittedly, had been broken into recently with cash, spirits and cigarettes being stolen. It was better to be safe than sorry, was father's view. The alarm was modern and fairly sophisticated. It operated on two levels. When activated the main doors were wired so that the alarm would go off when they were opened. And each room had a small, box-like device which reacted to movement. A small red light came on sensing somebody nearby and this happened whether the alarm was switched on or not. It gave great peace of mind.

The first time the alarm went off was the day I had fixed up some mobiles in the main bar area advertising soft drinks. It was part of an attempt to make the large pub with its mainly bare walls look reasonably attractive. It was a Saturday and father and I had gone to the rugby league match and we had dropped mother and the girls off in Calderthorpe to do some shopping. It was a close day and one of the large front windows was partially open to cool the place down a little. The mobiles were my idea. Opening the window was my mother's.

We activated the alarm, locked up and left. It must have been seconds after the car left the car park that one of the mobiles, moved by the draught, was sensed by the little black box with the little red light and off went the alarm. The efficiency of our local police station was put to the test and neighbours told us that they were there within two or three minutes. One young bobby climbed in through the open window and searched the premises only to find our all too friendly dog that licked his hand. Whisky – a guard dog he wasn't – was another reason for fitting a burglar alarm.

The police could find no way of turning the alarm off save sending for the company that fitted it, which they did. We arrived home to a rather curt note from the Inspector in charge of the local station to contact him. Father rang him and received an earful about checking such things as windows when leaving the premises empty. 'Burglar alarms are all very well Mister Lowe, but they don't make up for stupid actions.'

Father was furious and waded into mother and me. Naturally I got the brunt for putting up the mobiles, mother claiming that they would have moved around even with the window closed. There was little point in arguing so I took them down resolving not to be helpful in future.

A few months later my parents had taken the two girls for a long weekend break to the Lake District. Norman and I were running the pub. It was Friday night and we had turned out the last of the customers and were settling down for a staff drink when there was a knock on the front door. In came two raw young constables in an affable enough mood.

'Everything all right sir?' they asked Norman who responded by pointing to me and saying that I was 'Sir'. They were possibly a little thrown by my youth. 'You're Mister Lowe,' – the 'sir' was a little late in coming this time.

I explained that I was but that my father was the licensee. 'We're just having a staff drink officers, would you care to join us?' They hesitated but, when the slightly older one gave the nod, accepted.

I pulled them two halves of bitter and they parked their helmets on the bar top. We chatted and they seemed a pair of decent lads. One of them kept eyeing the small black box with its occasional winking red light.

'Do you mind me asking,' – the 'sir' was dropped completely now – 'what that little device is?'

Norman jumped in. 'It's our new burglar alarm,' he said. 'And when that red light comes on it's taking a photograph so that we know exactly what is happening when the pub is shut. If someone breaks in we have a picture of them. It's quite sophisticated. We'd switched it on just before you came in.'

The policemen were taken aback. One placed his helmet over his half pint of beer, the other turned his face away from what he thought was the camera lens. They suddenly developed a desire to

"Do you mind me asking what that little device is?"

be on their way. 'Must go now, sir' – it was back – 'other premises to visit.'

We were having great difficulty in keeping our faces straight when Brian Dyson broke out into a fit of laughter and the rest of us followed.

The bobbies were mystified, then one of them twigged it. 'You're having us on,' he said.

'Of course!' we chorused. 'Have another drink,' I said.

'Better not,' said one of the policemen.

'Evening all,' said Brian.

🍺 🍺 🍺 🍺 🍺 🍺 🍺 🍺 🍺

Relations with the police were pretty good. In the five years that my family kept the Coach and Four, apart from the burglar alarm incident, I can only remember one cross word from the Superintendent who commanded the Oldford division of the West Riding Constabulary. That was about under age drinking, an enduring problem that affects most licensees. In those days there were no identity cards and landlords had to trust their own judgement. Sixteen-year-olds, particularly well made lads and well made-up girls, often looked to be twenty and unless you knew them and their age it was difficult to challenge them. It was possible to refuse to serve them but turning away trade is not in the landlord's long-term best interest.

The law doesn't help either in allowing fourteen-year-olds and above into pubs provided they don't purchase or consume alcohol. A group of young people would come in and sit in a corner, order a round including one or two soft drinks, and happily booze away all evening. If anyone of them were challenged then they would claim the soft drink was theirs. And the close proximity of Calderthorpe meant that Oldford had the problem of that town's under age drinkers and the pubs there had ours. Being careful just wasn't enough.

The police had decided to clamp down and mid-evening one Saturday all the local pubs got visits without warning.

'Just looking round Mister Lowe,' said the Superintendent.

We had obviously drawn the short straw. He was accompanied

by our old friend Sergeant Powell and it was soon clear enough what they were after. In the corner of the concert room was a crowd of six or seven youngsters. Bert Powell rooted out three of them straight away. The lemonade trick didn't work with him having seen it all before.

'Sharing it between three of you, are you? Whilst the others have two drinks each.'

They found three more in other parts of the pub, one of whom was a six foot lad only just turned fifteen whom I had served several times before. The Superintendent told my father that he had seen him playing for Oldford Cricket Club's under 15s side a couple of weeks ago.

No action followed but the Superintendent called a meeting of the town's licensees and gave them the hard word on under-age drinking. He was not going to tolerate it. They had it in their hands to stop it and any further breaches would be followed by prosecution.

After the meeting he called my father to one side and said that he had been very lucky not to have ended up in court because there had been more illegal drinkers found at the Coach and Four than any other pub in the town. Dad pleaded innocence but the Super wasn't having any. 'One more slip, Mister Lowe, and I'll come down on you like a ton of bricks.'

The old man was angry when he returned to the pub claiming he'd been let down by the police and by his staff.

'Why us?' we chorused.

Reflecting he said: 'OK, but we'll all have to be ultra careful from now on. Anyone who looks under 21 must be challenged and if you're not satisfied then make the blighters produce their birth certificate or passport or something. Otherwise no service.'

From then on there was seldom any trouble; the odd Calderthorpe youth would attempt to get service but generally the kids themselves seemed to have taken note. We learned that the police had been putting the message about in the high schools and youth clubs and whatever they had been saying seemed to have had its effect.

After hours drinking was not a problem at the Coach and Four. Coming, as he did, from being steward of a working men's club on the Lancashire holiday coast, father knew a few things about emptying licensed premises at closing time. He also knew that his licence was on the line if he allowed it to go on. The police in Oldford took a lenient view. They knew what was going on most of the time and cases of regular 'lates' were jumped on informally, the licensee warned and, hopefully, that was the end of it. A blind eye was turned for the odd case with the police themselves often taking advantage of the landlord's amiability.

Customers often fail to realise that staying behind for a late drink or two is merely extending the licensee's working day.

'I can just see the bank manager or the librarian staying open after their closing time, and that wouldn't be breaking the law,' father proclaimed.

He accepted that, particularly at weekends, staff were entitled to a drink in some reasonable comfort. They were not encouraged to drink whilst working and dad felt it better to wait until the punters had departed. Occasionally favoured friends like the Smithies would be asked to stay for what Norman called a 'lock-in'.

During his tenancy father was careful enough and to some extent fortunate not to get into any trouble over out of hours drinking at the Coach and Four. But he did manage to do so at the Oldford British Legion Club where occasionally he and Bert Cox would pop round for a game of snooker on weekday afternoons. The Legion opened at three and was a popular watering hole for retired blokes and those who could arrange their own working hours. It was always assumed that the afternoon opening, permitted for clubs, was in order. In fact it wasn't. Several clubs in the town had similar hours and no one had told their secretaries and committee men that the law had been changed just after the war and a fresh application for other than the regular licensing hours should have been submitted each year.

The regular Superintendent of Police was on leave and an unpopular and ambitious Chief Inspector was in charge of the division and anxious to make himself known. He hovered about the pubs but everyone was on their mettle. For those two weeks no one parked out of place and even the local villains confined their activities to the surrounding towns. It must have been a frustrating time for him. However he didn't give up and in his survey of the local records found out that most of the clubs in Oldford had licences that only allowed opening during the standard hours – those used by the pubs.

This was the Chief Inspector's opportunity. Friday was a busy day in the clubs and armed with the appropriate warrants he went off with a sergeant and two constables to do his worst. First stop was the British Legion and there, much to everyone's surprise he closed down the bar, confiscated everyone's drinks and warned that summonses would follow. More than 40 men including my father and Bert were involved. His next stop was the Conservative Club and it was here that he got his greatest haul. Not that there were more than at the Legion but in the quality of those caught drinking outside permitted hours – for that was what they were doing.

A week earlier a prominent local politician had died. Alderman George Pickersgill was a pillar of the Conservative party in the West Riding. He had been a member of the county council and Mayor of Oldford on two occasions. The funeral that day had been quite a big affair. Political differences had been put aside and a number of members of all parties on the Oldford Borough Council had gone to pay their respects to Alderman George. Afterwards, as is the way with these things, quite a few had retired to the 'Con' club. Along with all the prominent Conservatives they included the Labour leader and two former Labour Mayors and a Liberal member who was the parliamentary candidate for the Oldford constituency and several Justices of the Peace as well. The Chief Inspector nabbed the lot and the press had a heyday.

The funeral was reported well down the page in the Oldford Weekly Clarion. It had to be to make room for headlines such as: 'Top Labour Men in Tory Club Raid'. It followed the Tuesday morning sitting of the Oldford magistrates' court where 80 or so worthies were each fined two pounds for drinking outside licensing hours in the British Legion Club and the Conservative Club. The Chief Inspector had not got round to the two working mens' clubs. Some officials were fined ten pounds each and given what appeared to be a tongue in cheek warning as to their future conduct.

One man was missing from the bench that morning. Councillor Bernard Roberts JP was the chairman of the Oldford magistrates and he, too, had been at the funeral of his good friend.

It had been his suggestion that a drink at George's club would be a nice gesture. He was also fined two pounds. So very few noticed the names of two of the town's licensees amongst those who were fined that day. They were well down the list and small fry in such distinguished company.

Two weeks later the two clubs received official notification that they could open at 3 p.m. after making a proper application. On the same day a certain Chief Inspector was given a sideways move to Sedbergh in that tiny enclave of the West Riding that is almost in the Lake District and a long way from Oldford.

🍺🍺🍺🍺🍺🍺🍺🍺🍺🍺

My father had to appear in court one day to apply for an occasional licence. Normally he would arrange such things in good time and the matter would be dealt with formally but it was a late booking for a christening party and he was unable to give the appropriate notice.

The chairman of the local bench that day was a teetotaller and instead of allowing licensing matters to take precedence he put them to the end of the list and father and a couple of other licensees had to sit for most of the morning while the detritus of Oldford's petty crime was given summary jurisdiction.

Among those half dozen or so charged with drunkenness was Ozzy Pendlebury, a well known local layabout who was banned in most of Oldford's pubs. He had apparently bought a couple of bottles of British Wine in Calderthorpe and together with his mate, George Phillips who had a quart of cider, had proceeded on a bender of gigantic proportions. They had probably had three or four pints in Ma Gamp's at lunchtime as she wasn't too particular about her customers – anything for a milk stout.

They were picked up near the canal bridge in the mid evening after complaints of them singing (sic) and causing a general nuisance. Phillips was fined ten shillings, the usual amount for such an offence, and given the regular warnings. Then up popped Ozzy as large as life. He attended the court much more frequently than his colleague and thought he knew the ropes. He pleaded guilty and when the chairman, regarding him with disdain, asked if he had anything to say for himself Ozzy replied that yesterday had been his birthday and 'your honour' would know how it was on such occasions. 'Your honour' obviously didn't know and fined Ozzy one pound without consulting his fellow justices.

On another occasion Ozzy was before the bench on a drunk and disorderly charge after consuming, he claimed, twelve pints of Harrison's Best. He caught another sanctimonious chairman who proceeded to give him a lecture on the perils of alcohol and the delights of drinking water: 'You ought to drink water, Mister Pendlebury,' he intoned. This took Ozzy back a bit for no one had ever called him Mister Pendlebury before. 'Water makes horses and lions strong,' wound up the magistrate.

Ozzy was no man to be put down by a teetotaller: 'Have they never heard of 'Arrison's?' he snapped back.

The local police were having some bother with forged one pound notes. From what Sergeant Powell told my father they were being made locally and were very professionally done, even to the extent of having a metal strip through them and serial numbers not following an obvious sequence. Locally meant, probably, Bradford or Leeds where most of those discovered so far had turned up.

We were briefed by father who liked to remind us that he had been in the Corps of Military Police during the war. (He was probably the smallest MP and spent most of his time directing traffic through North Africa and up into Italy – he was certainly no Philip Marlowe.) All we knew was that the colouring of the notes was a tiny bit paler than the usual ones and the metal strips were 'a little uncertain in their settings', whatever that may have meant. On each till a genuine note was fixed to allow immediate comparisons to be made.

It was OK during the week when trade was none too busy but at weekends it was difficult to check every note. 'Never mind,' said Norman, 'If we get some forgeries in and don't spot them, then perhaps we'll have passed them on come closing time.' In fact that was just what we didn't do.

It was only when we closed after a formidably busy Saturday night and my mother was counting the takings that a forged note turned up. But there was only one and naturally nobody could remember who took it let alone where it came from. But the police were called in and they took the offending note away leaving Dad moaning all day Sunday that he was a quid down in his takings.

As it turned out several were passed in the town that Saturday evening, but unfortunately none were noticed at the time by bar staff. The following lunchtime Brian Dyson spotted one when a young bloke, not a regular, bought a round with what turned out to be a dodgy note. He quietly put it to one side and rang the police. A CID inspector came round and the customer was pointed out by Brian. His story was that he had probably got the note in his last week's pay packet.

Over the next two or three weeks the notes continued to appear. I had one passed to me by an eminently respectable woman and I earned the approbation of my father by giving it straight back to her and pointing out that it was probably a forgery and that she ought to show it to the police. The old man was fed up with the police hanging on to what he termed: 'Half my takings'. They actually had three one pound notes taken at the Coach and Four but, as father also said: 'As we're helping them (the police) do their work, I don't see why we should pay for the privilege.'

Some smart police work traced the tracks of the forgers by the clues passed on from the staff of pubs, shops and the like. It was a gang of four, two of whom were master printers and another an expert engraver. They operated from a warehouse in Bradford and had printed some three thousand one pound notes of a very high quality indeed. They had a smooth operation to launder them into the money market.

The four came up for trial at Leeds Quarter Sessions, were found guilty and received long jail sentences. Our local bobbies received special praise from the judge for what he called 'patient and exhaustive detective work'. He also complimented local folk in Oldford for their co-operation. My father said words were all very well but he was still three quid out on the deal.

THE MUSICIAN'S TALE

*"All music is folk music, I ain't never heard
no horse sing a song."*
LOUIS ARMSTRONG

RUNNING A PUB ISN'T AS SIMPLE AS IT seems. The people in charge have to be experts in the provision of good service for food, drink and entertainment. It was not enough just to be an innkeeper in a small town pub in the years after the war; quite a lot more was expected. The landlord must also be an impresario or the clubs would take over. He also needed to be a psychiatrist and to anticipate what would please his customers. And there were times when he would make a mistake.

He was the worst comedian I had ever heard. Where father got him from I shudder to think. Even the blue jokes were a decade old and most of his gags were the sort my sisters brought home from school and tried out on me. The 'Why did the chicken cross the road?' variety. And for the first time in my life I was hearing so-called racist jokes. Most of the customers were ignoring him and carrying on their own conversations. Unlike working men's clubs where a strict chairman would be imploring: '...best of order please, comedian on his feet...' there was nobody in a pub to call for silence.

He staggered on and there was a blessed relief when he finished his piece and my father took the opportunity to pay the man off and suggest that he better not do his second spot. He slipped a couple of pounds to Ronnie Taylor to do an hour on the piano and it was a welcome exchange.

Picking the right turns was only one of the problems. Picking the right audience was another. Father put on live entertainment on Fridays and Saturdays as did most of the bigger local pubs. On those evenings there might be thirty or forty entertainers of various sorts working the clubs and pubs of Oldford. Television was in its infancy and we were still in the period of the variety theatre – the Alhambra in Calderthorpe attracted some of the best artistes in Britain. The clubs would band together to bring big names into the area for a series of weekend shows. There was a lot of competition.

Pubs were at the back of the entertainers' address books. The stage paid best, then the clubs, finally the pubs. But to keep a pub full you needed live music or a comedian, or both. Finding them was difficult, particularly with the limited budgets landlords had. The managers were in a worse position than tenants because they had to rely on the generosity of the brewery for an entertainment allowance. Word would go around that a good singer was about at a reasonable price and a phone call would secure them. There was little enough time to go out and test the waters as the concert secretaries from the clubs would do. You took a chance.

Saturday night audiences were different to any other night of the week. It was the night when people 'went out'. Not to their local but to pubs some miles away either by car or, more often in those days, by bus. On Saturdays at the Coach and Four our custom was made up of three groups: we got a hard core of local regulars, another group of regulars who came from further afield just for that evening, and the casuals who had either heard of the pub or of the entertainer and who simply dropped in. In total they demanded a better standard of entertainment than on other nights of the week when there were mainly only local regulars about.

Fortunately it was a Friday when the dreadful comedian was on and what most of the audience required was a background noise – a ballad singer or a pianist. A comedian would have to be very good to live long in that company. This particular one couldn't even attract a response to his '...my dog's got no nose.... how does it smell?... bloody awful...' routine. If he had been there on a Saturday he would have taken a knock-out in round one.

Father had booked him on the say so of another landlord who

it turned out had the sense of humour of a member of the Waffen SS and the morals as well. His opinions were worth avoiding in future. For the Saturday bookings a group of us would often trail across West Yorkshire to working men's clubs looking for reasonably priced turns. Sunday night was the time to do this. The pub was quiet and my father was able to take a couple of hours off. Norman, Brian and I would accompany him along with Ronnie Taylor our resident pianist.

Ronnie was blind, having taken a bullet across the face in North Africa in 1942. He often made what appeared to be an obvious remark by saying that it had changed his life. But it was not just the blindness he was talking about. From being a labourer on building sites before the war he returned to civilian life to become a teacher of the physically handicapped and a more than competent pianist. 'I might be blind Wilf, but I lead a much fuller life than I would ever have done with sight,' he once told me.

He could play anything from Hoagy Carmichael to Frederick Chopin and the only music lessons he had were to train him as a piano tuner. Ronnie and his wife Diana lived opposite the pub in a canalside cottage and both were regulars, Ronnie more regular than most. He played for pleasure in the Coach and Four provided he could choose his own programme. He only demanded payment if my father dictated what type of music was to be played.

'Commercialism,' Ronnie would snort, breaking into a delightful medley of Gershwin, Kern and Berlin. He would often play exactly the same when he was doing his 'pleasure' bit but he had the freedom to break into a Beethoven sonata if he wished to.

Ronnie called himself my father's 'concert secretary' and took it upon himself to select and book most of the musical acts for the pub. He produced a group of five young men who did all sorts of amusing things with a variety of instruments. They called themselves, with disarming simplicity: The Comic Band. They were great and the customers that Saturday night were reluctant to let them go. We asked them to stay behind for a drink and discovered that this had been only their third booking. Dad made another booking for three months on and we wished them well.

Ronnie was less obvious than usual around the pub in the next few weeks. He would do his regular spot in the early part of

Saturday evening and was always available for the Sunday night talent spotting trips. But he missed out on some of the other sessions when he might have been expected to be there. Nobody questioned him – why should they?

Three months on and The Comic Band were set to return. They were becoming well known in the area and it was obviously going to be a popular evening. Extra bar staff had been drafted in. Ronnie asked my father if he could be excused his opening spot as he had something personal to attend to. That was fine as another regular known as 'Jolly Alice', a laughing, pudding of a lass, would pound the ivories in the style of Winifred Attwell for a couple of rums and peps.

The band turned up with Ronnie in tow. They had a more professional appearance than before and their fee had gone up slightly but their performance lacked nothing and was slicker and even funnier than the last time. The audience loved them. Again they were asked to stay behind and again father wanted to book them.

It was Ronnie who intervened. 'When do you want them Alex, because they're tied up all summer.' He was now their agent and had secured them a seasonal booking at one of the big clubs in Blackpool. They agreed to come back to the Coach and Four after the illuminations were dimmed in November.

Ronnie didn't go full time with the group but he had the fore-thought to recognise their talent and the know-how to put them on the road to success and he guided them through their early days. Their next performance at the Coach and Four was a knock-out but it was also their last one at that venue. They were now thoroughly professional and had already secured bookings for pantomime and another season at Blackpool but this time in one of the big shows. Ronnie continued to handle them for two more years and in doing so made quite a bit of money but they had now become such big names that their management needed to be with them and Ronnie was not for leaving Oldford and what he called 'the day job'.

My parents still get Christmas cards signed 'The Comic Band', although the group's name has long since changed. They remain top entertainers who remember their roots. Ronnie, years on, continues to play the piano in the Coach and Four and occasionally makes forays into the now lesser world of club life in the search for another star turn.

One of Ronnie's favourite tricks was to start off a sing-song with the audience going fit to burst. All the old stuff: Daisy, My Old Man, She was a Sweet Little Dicky Bird, My Girl's a Yorkshire Girl; then suddenly he would move into Beethoven's Moonlight Sonata with a look on his face as if he had been playing such stuff all night. Generally speaking the punters loved it.

One man, noted for his lack of a sense of humour, had other views. He held that Ronnie was taking the Mickey out of the crowd and patronising them and one night, when Ronnie called out for requests, he called out for some obscure piece of Chopin which apparently stumped the resident pianist. Some wag invited him to 'hum it and Ronnie will pick it up,' but there was no response. Ronnie appeared to take little notice.

The man tried it on with Ronnie a couple of times more but failed to spot that the effects were wearing thin with the audience. On the fourth and last time he called out: 'Play some Bach,' whilst making his way to the toilets. He had a silly grin on his face. On his return, the smirk was still there and as he walked across the room someone must have tipped off Ronnie. The pianist turned to his protagonist and said: 'Was it you that wanted Bach?'

Taken aback the man grunted affirmatively. 'Would you prefer something by Johann Sebastian Bach, Carl Phillip Emmanuel Bach, Wilhelm Friedemann Bach or perhaps one of the others?' and without waiting for an answer moved smoothly into his own arrangement of one of the Brandenburg concertos.

🍷 🍷 🍷 🍷 🍷 🍷 🍷 🍷 🍷 🍷

One of the most popular of the Saturday night turns was a husband and wife team of singers – tenor and soprano – who could trot out all the popular musical comedy favourites as well as songs from the more recent musicals such as Oklahoma, Carousel and My Fair Lady. If Georgette and Wilfred Percival – accompanied, of course, by Dolly at the piano – were advertised to play at the Coach and Four then you needed to arrive early to get a seat.

The Percivals were from Leeds and had been around for some

years. Pre-war they had been professionals on the halls with summer seasons at Scarborough, Filey or Bridlington but since 1945, when competition had become fierce, they were making a comfortable living around the clubs and pubs of the West Riding without having to leave their home. A Saturday night appearance for our pub would have to be shared with another venue in Oldford – business is business.

But they were good box office and ensured a busy night wherever they played. The trouble with the Percivals was that they were such awful snobs. They earned their living those days in the pubs and clubs but made it clear that they regarded it as far below their dignity. They expected to be treated like royalty and demanded a dressing room. My mother had to prepare her bedroom for them because it was the only one with a wash basin in it and they still complained that there were no 'en suite' facilities. Despite having a car they often wanted a taxi on hand to take them to their next venue and one of the landlords was expected to pick up the tab. And they treated poor Dolly like a slave.

*The trouble with the Percivals was
that they were such awful snobs*

She took it all with equanimity. I was fond of her and got quite pally with her particularly during the long periods it took for the Percivals to change into, what Norman Dyson called, their 'Viennese Opera Ball attire'. Dolly told me how they objected to driving across Leeds to pick her up and often made her travel to the city centre by bus to meet them. She didn't object for she was reasonably well paid and the work was regular. But she did insist on being taken home.

Dolly had a habit that did not endear her to the Percivals. When playing the piano she was a chain smoker. At other times she smoked the occasional cigarette but when she played she fumed continuously. The packet was open on top of the piano and a fag drooped from the corner of her mouth. Taking her left hand off the bass she would extract her next smoke from the packet whilst the right hand continued the accompaniment. She would place the cigarette in the opposite corner of her mouth then withdraw the old one and light up from it. And so on. She even appeared to have the ability to time the completion of her smoke to the end of a musical selection.

She got through about sixty a night and the Percivals could do nothing about it for they were fully occupied giving vent to Gilbert and Sullivan or Rogers and Hammerstein. No sweet little Buttercup, Dolly, but she certainly walked alone.

Georgette – she was Polly Sykes before she married him, said Dolly – would remonstrate between pieces but always with a fixed smile on her face because she had her public to consider. What she didn't know was that it didn't matter one jot and the drinkers regarded Dolly's eccentricities as part of the show.

My father had booked the Percivals for a Saturday evening in the run up to Christmas and it was expected to be a busy night. Wilfred phoned in mid week to say they were having problems because they had lost what he called their accompanist. 'Dolly's gone?' said father, 'Why?'

Wilfred was reluctant to expand, saying they had decided to part company. Would our regular pianist be prepared to support them?

Father explained that Ronnie was blind, self taught and played by ear; good enough for sing-alongs and his own interpretations, but not for the Percivals. Couldn't they find somebody else?

It seemed not. The truth was that they were such difficult folk to get along with that nobody wanted to play with them. Dolly had started with them in 1935 and, apart from during Wilfred's war service, had been with them until now. Father reluctantly allowed them to break their contract and just before ringing off he asked for Dolly's address. Wilfred blustered but eventually gave it to him.

My father had an idea and he phoned me at my digs in Leeds and asked if that evening I would call on Dolly and ask her to do the spot on Saturday. I eventually found her house on a large council estate and she was delighted to see me and to accept the booking. Someone though would have to fetch her and could we put her up for the night?

Of course we could do both and the date was fixed. At that stage I made no inquiries as to why she had split with the Percivals – Saturday night would be soon enough.

Dolly was a knock-out, playing all of the duet's songs but encouraging the audience to join in. She was double quick in lighting one cigarette from another, not having the singers for continuity, and it seemed her rate of smoking increased. The crowd loved her and she was delighted that she may have found a new career. My father shared in the pleasures of the evening not least in the amount of money that had passed through the tills.

Afterwards we entertained Dolly to supper and a few drinks. The Coach and Four, she said, was always one of her favourite venues because folk there treated her decently and didn't ignore her whilst falling for the bluff of the Percivals. Good entertainers that they were, they had forgotten their roots and as they got older they would begin to recognise that their talents wouldn't last forever. Some philosopher, Dolly. But why had they split up?

It happened in a working men's club in Bradford. Dolly was giving her all to a selection from The King and I, puffing away contentedly when, for the first time ever, she failed to do a clean change of cigarette. The lit one fell from her fingers on to the key board and in sweeping it to the floor Dolly struck a confusion of wrong notes at which the Percivals displayed a surprising lack of professionalism and lost their musical way. After a few seconds that seemed like minutes, said Dolly, they got it together and while the audience had a good laugh the singers were most embarrassed.

She got through about sixty a night

In reality it was a minor incident but Georgette determined not to see it that way. Immediately the selection finished she swept over to the piano and started to remonstrate with Dolly saying she had seen this coming for years what with her smoking and it would have to stop.

But Dolly was a match for her and had been waiting for this opportunity. 'That's enough,' she cried. 'I'm fed up with your carping and complaining. I've trailed around after you two for years watching you imagine you were playing to royalty when you were at some scruffy club and treating me like dirt. I'm off.' And turning to the concert secretary she asked him if he'd be kind enough to get her a taxi to Leeds. Dolly gathered up her music and left. Wilfred tried to smooth things over but it was no use.

My father broke off from laughing at the thoughts of the remainder of that evening to say that Dolly could drop her lighted fag ends on his piano any evening she liked so long as she played like she did tonight. I wondered about how our resident pianist

Ronnie felt about things but need not have worried. They had entirely different styles and repertoires and the next time Dolly came to the Coach and Four they were persuaded to play a duet which went down well. We didn't see much more of Dolly because of where she lived and the fact that she had no transport. But she built up her contacts in the Leeds area and never ceased to thank my old man for thinking of her and giving her the chance to break out on her own.

🕊 🕊 🕊 🕊 🕊 🕊 🕊 🕊 🕊 🕊

The parish church of St Wilfred was next but one to the Coach and Four. I thought it entirely appropriate that my given name should be that of a saint and along with my mother if not regular worshippers at the parish church we were the most consistent of the family. For one thing I enjoyed a good sing as did my mother and we were both occasional members of the choir.

The vicar, the Rev Charles A Catterall MA, was a homely, if pompous, old soul, well past retirement but carrying on until younger men were ready to take over. Like many other professions the priesthood had been severely cut in numbers by the war. He was not one for the drink and, so far as we knew, had never been in the Coach. But he was civil enough to us and my mother always supported church charities and fund raising events and he was appreciative.

The choir master, a rumbustious fellow called Harry Parkinson, who was possessed of one of the best tenor voices in Yorkshire, enjoyed his pint of Best and along with a dozen or so mixed voices would usually have a drink in the Coach after choir practice and often on Sunday lunch times. Harry had been in the Huddersfield Choral Society for some years and his great ambition was to 'do a Messiah' at Oldford. But Mister Catterall thought otherwise.

His line was that it was all right for the Huddersfield Choral Society with the backing of such famous orchestras as the Hallé and the Royal Liverpool Philharmonic but St Wilfred's church choir and Philip Evans on the organ would be demeaning. Harry tried to explain that he would enhance the cast, so to speak, for the occasion. But the vicar was adamant.

Without asking anyone I suggested to Harry Parkinson that the pub might be a good place to stage the Messiah. The concert room held about 200 folk if the tables were taken out and the small stage could be extended to house the choir, soloists and the Oldford Prize Band. We would have to do without the organ but there was a piano. He was interested.

I needed to talk to my father about it and wondered what his reaction would be. First I had a roundabout conversation with my mother who was lukewarm, although I suspected she would want to be in the show if it came off. But she said I would have to convince my father first.

'What do you think this place is, a flipping opera house?' was his first comment. 'It's a public house where men can sit and talk and think,' he went on quoting some half remembered text that I was sure was something to do with temperance but I was reluctant to point this out.

'And drink?' I posed.

'Yes, and drink,' he said 'and a fat lot of ale we'll sell with a pub full of bible bashers.'

I tried the placatory approach. Handel, so far as I knew was not tee-total, neither were most of the choir and none of the band – it's almost a condition of membership that trumpet players sup ale, I suggested. The audience likewise in going to a pub to hear good music and good singing would almost certainly buy drinks if only soft ones. 'And those are the ones you make most profit on,' I pointed out. There would be three opportunities to sell drinks – before and after the performance and during the interval and we were talking about 200 plus customers. Not, I implied, to be sneezed at.

He was worn down eventually by my mother who picked up where I had left off and said that such an occasion would be good for the reputation of the pub and might bring in a few customers who would stay to become regulars. The economic arguments usually prevailed with dad. Customers he could always do with.

To avoid upsetting the vicar, Harry Parkinson decided to call the choir the Oldford Choral Society and placed no obligation on present members to take part in the performance. He called in a favour from an old pal of his to conduct the Messiah and decided to take the solo tenor part himself. The choir had a good soprano and the other two soloists were borrowed from a Bradford society with, again, Harry calling in favours. A few members of other local church choirs also joined in. The band was delighted to take part, although many questioned their ability to cope with such a major work.

'They're OK with Colonel Bogey and the like,' said Norman one evening, 'but let them loose on the Hallelujah Chorus and the lord have mercy on their souls; or maybe on ours.' He had other worries too but they were not confined to this particular show. 'Whenever I see or hear the Messiah I chuckle to myself at those busty spinsters and matronly ladies of a certain age bellowing out: 'For unto us a child is born. I'm sure George Frederick Handel didn't have that in mind when he wrote it.' His comments were taken in good humour by Harry Parkinson who roped him in for two guineas to be a patron.

Rehearsals were held in the Methodist church hall by courtesy of the Minister who was a good friend of the pub and who encouraged his flock to attend. Tickets at five shillings each were soon sold out and before the event there was talk of a second performance.

'Let's get this one out of the way first,' said Harry.

The band, despite Norman's misgivings, was playing well and certainly enjoying themselves. The only complaint was that it was a fair walk from the rehearsal room to the Coach and Four.

The event was fixed for a Tuesday evening and the final rehearsal was in the pub that afternoon. The local papers had picked up on what they considered to be a unique occasion and during the previous weekend Harry Parkinson had been in great demand for interviews, as had my father who gave the impression that he had favoured the idea from the start. My mother who overheard him pressured him into buying her a new hat. 'A hat! Just to sing in!' exploded father. But he gave in.

It was a famous evening. It was not the best performance ever given but must have ranked as one of the most enjoyable for those of us who sang and played and for those who listened. The great choruses were given a new dimension.

Even father was delighted. 'I've not taken so much on Tuesday night in the five years I've been in the pub,' he said, 'And I enjoyed the music.'

....

'Hallelujah it's a pub!' was the headline of the piece in the Yorkshire Echo and 'Handel to a pint pot of Harrison's Best' was the witty way the Calderthorpe Echo (incorporating the Oldford Bugle) summed it up. A few weeks later there was a short laudatory article in the St Wilfred's parish magazine. With hardly anyone noticing him the vicar had slipped in and out of the performance for his one and only visit to the pub.

THE EPILOGUE – MOVING ON

*"The moving finger writes; and, having writ,
Moves on"*
THE RUBÁIYÁT OF OMAR KHAYYÁM EDWARD FITZGERALD

IT WAS TIME TO MOVE ON. My father and mother had been at the Coach and Four for more than five years and the feeling that this was about long enough was shared by all of us. There were other reasons too. My mother felt a change in style was necessary. She wanted a smaller pub with some opportunity to show off her cooking. Sandwiches and pies were the usual fare at the Coach but she had higher ambitions. And there was the threat of a take-over by one of the big brewers hanging over Harrison's which would almost certainly mean the closing of the brewery. A lot of landlords including my father were feeling uncomfortable because of it.

With the girls in mind it was not a bad time to move either. Jane was just finishing her 'O' levels and if she was going to stay on at school a change of base at this stage would not harm her very much. Wendy was still two years away from examinations and could also absorb the move. And I had had about enough. It had been a novelty spending most weekends and holidays in a pub and the extra cash that came from working there was useful, but enough was enough and I wanted out, to do my own thing, develop my career and perhaps get married.

Father, in his usual manner, was prepared to go along with the majority view particularly after the rest of us had persuaded him that it was his idea in the first place. So my folks started to look for another pub.

....

They fancied a free house in the Yorkshire Dales and reckoned they could just about scrape together enough to buy one. It was a buyer's market at that time and the choice was wide enough. I was happy to play my part in helping to search out a suitable place but I had made up my mind that my visits to the new place would not be so regular and I had already taken steps to buy a flat in Leeds.

Over the Whitsun holiday we travelled through Wharfedale and into Swaledale; we went up Nidderdale and down Ribblesdale; we scoured Teesdale and combed Wensleydale. I thought about taking up geography as my main subject. There was no part of the Yorkshire Dales that the Lowes did not visit during that peach of a summer. Yet it was less than ten miles from the Coach and Four that my family found exactly what they were looking for.

Facing the green of a pretty little mill village on the Lancashire border stood the Wordsworths' Inn – the apostrophe's position was important. It was stone built around 1790 and was distinguished by a splendid sign showing the poet William Wordsworth flanked by his wife, Mary, and his ever faithful sister, Dorothy. They had stayed there on one of their many perambulations. The sign had been painted by a local Royal Academician more than a century ago and was well preserved.

Inside was a tiny tap room frequented, so it seemed, by half a dozen octogenarians. The comfortable and spacious lounge opened out into a dining area which seated about twenty. There were four bedrooms and a small flatlet with its own entrance. The kitchen was adequate and there was a laundry (dad called it the wash-house) and my mother was delighted. The girls loved it and there were suitable schools nearby. Father was already planning which beers to sell. And it also got my approval although no one seemed bothered by this.

The price was just above my father's limit but the agent indicated that haggling was possible. The present owners were approaching 70 and wanted to spend their evening years enjoying the benefits of their labours. Mister Green, a large man who laughed a lot, said that these days he was built for comfort not speed. His wife, who I never heard speak, nodded agreement.

My father decided to borrow a small sum of money from the bank rather than accept the cheaper rates of the brewers with the ties involved. Harrison's in particular had been keen to lend him money. But he made his own arrangements and by the end of July the deal was struck.

They were to move in at the beginning of September – perfect timing. Back at the Coach and Four there was a more relaxed air than usual so I suggested that mother and father and the two girls should take a holiday. They had not had more than two or three days off together since we moved there. I said that, with the help of Norman, I could cope. Surprisingly they agreed and Norman's wife Mary, who managed a travel agency in Calderthorpe, fixed up the tickets.

They took the car to Ireland, crossing from Liverpool to Dublin, and for two weeks visited the places in the west they had trekked to on bicycles on their honeymoon in the year before I was born. They all had a marvellous time, particularly the girls who both fell in love with the same black-eyed lad from Kerry. Father told the tale with great gusto of how he asked a landlord when did his pub close and was told: 'October'. It did them all a world of good. It was more than could be said for those of us back at the ranch.

In the first place the word got around that the Lowe family had already left the Coach and Four. So there was an influx of the unsavoury crowd that had difficulty getting served in decent pubs – trying it on with a new landlord. They got short shrift from Norman. There was even a visit from some of the Quality Street gang who, fortunately, we had not seen since the early days. They were treated with cold respect and served but they soon realised that the rumours were just that – rumours.

Then there was the day that the roof fell in. Not, I'm glad to say, the roof of the pub but the one over the garages at the back of the car park. Hughie and Tommy, the genial Ulstermen who used to lodge with us still used the loft as a store for the tinned goods they sold on the markets. There was access by an external staircase and it seemed that in a hurry one evening they had brought up lots of cases and stored them all at the near end, over the first garage – the one that I used.

I heard a rumbling in the night but dismissed it as thunder. The outward appearance of the garage showed nothing untoward. It was only after breakfast when I opened the door to get at my car that I discovered what had happened. I was almost submerged but I managed to jump clear in time. There was my precious 1938

Morris Ten covered in rubble and what seemed like a million tins of baked beans. I could see into the store room and the floor had collapsed across all six garages. Fortunately there was only one other car there and that belonged to Hughie, one of the culprits. If indeed, they were the culprits for I suspected that either the landlord or the brewery had a responsibility to maintain the property in good order.

But these thoughts did not disturb my mind for the moment. I was absolutely furious. It was my first car and I treated it like a beloved child. If either of those two blessed Irishmen were to have moved into sight at that moment I would cheerfully have thrown a tin of beans at them, or two, or maybe three. A crowd had formed and someone asked me what had happened.

'You can see what's bloody happened,' I cried. 'Some silly beggar's wrecked my car.' And I cried, not the tears of despondency or sadness but the tears of anger.

Norman and Mary Dyson arrived and Mary, ever practical, made a pot of tea. She was right of course but at the time I felt like drinking a bottle of brandy. We realised that some emergency service should be summoned but which?

'Are you in the AA or the RAC?' said a well-meaning friend.

'A fat lot of good a bloke on a motorbike with a sidecar would be in this situation,' retorted Norman. 'Better ring the Fire Brigade.'

Which I did, explaining that no one was hurt, only my feelings. They came along and managed to drag the car out. The bodywork was a complete write-off, consequently so was the car. Bob Smithies gave me ten pounds for it and towed it away to his garage. The local fire brigade shored up the garages after removing Hughie's car which, being near the far end, was hardly touched. I presented several cases of beans to the firemen and invited them for a drink.

'Save your money,' said the Sub Officer. 'We'll have to charge you for this.'

I thought that was the last straw until a Building Inspector arrived from the local council having been informed of the event by the Fire Brigade.

He picked his way around the rubble and expressed his satisfaction at the way it had been made safe. 'But it will have to be demolished of course,' he continued. 'It's a pretty expensive job but we'll give you 14 days to do it. Meanwhile no one must go nearer than ten yards from it and you'll have to rope off that area around the building.'

This meant we were going to lose more than half the car park. Good heavens what would the brewery say? What would my father say?

I decided that the family could wait and with a bit of luck the whole business could be sorted out by the time they returned. The brewery would have to be told at once and I phoned Jack Thornton. He was golfing but his wife said she would get a message to him at the club. The Smithies as usual turned up trumps and provided a makeshift fence around the garages. Norman meanwhile had opened the pub, which was doing an extraordinary amount of business. Nothing like tragedy, I thought, to set the tills ringing. It's a black day that has no silver lining, as one of those blessed Ulstermen might have said.

The next few days were frenetic. Jack Thornton was a tremendous help and agreed that the brewery would accept full responsibility for the Fire Brigade's bill and the demolition. He got things under way and the job was completed in four days. That also had its spin-off with the demolition gang spending a lot of their overtime earnings in the Coach and Four. I reckoned that father would be reasonably placated when he learned how the crisis had been dealt with.

There only remained my confrontation with Hughie and Tommy. On the day the roof fell in they had been in Stockton-on-Tees and didn't arrive back at the pub until early evening. Their usual pattern was to have a couple of pints of Guinness, load up for the following day, have a couple more pints and then, as the fancy took them, either go home to their digs or have a couple more pints. That evening they walked in with the jaunty air of men who had done well from the world. Their pockets jangled. I was upstairs having a meal and Norman manned the bar.

He served them and then told them what had happened. They both went white thinking at first that I had been hurt. Norman reassured them but told them that I was very angry, initially about the damage to my precious car but, on reflection, about the possibility that someone could have been injured. Norman came up to me and told me to take it calmly. The boys could not have been more apologetic and offered to buy me a replacement car. I told them that I had given away a load of their baked beans but it didn't worry them. Later we got happily stoated together and made jokes about tins of beans falling off the back of a fire engine.

We came close to another disaster whilst my family were on holiday. This time it wasn't the wrath of my father I would have experienced, although he would have been annoyed to say the least. It was Norman Dyson that I would have had to contend with because it happened, or nearly did, in his precious cellar.

One of the cleaners was on holiday and whilst the other one would normally cope on her own, she fell down the back steps of her house and badly sprained an ankle. So I drafted in Vera Brocklesby and her daughter Enid to help.

Enid usually brought her young son, Billy, a mischievous monkey of a lad, along with her. He wasn't malicious or destructive, just plain inquisitive. I caught him in the tap room once after he had emptied out all the boxes of dominoes and he told me he was counting the spots. As I regarded this as good for a primary school kid, I left him to it. On another occasion he had found father's stock of beer mats and was building houses with them. As I said, there was no real harm in him.

One morning I heard Enid calling out for Billy and she sounded concerned. I went downstairs into the bar area and asked her what was the matter.

'Billy's vanished,' she said. 'I've looked everywhere for him and can't find him nowhere.'

Vera went upstairs and I searched the yard and out-buildings while Enid went over her tracks again in the public rooms. He was not to be seen. Unless, I thought, he's in the cellar. Normally the door was kept locked but that morning I had been down for some bottles and had left it open as a delivery was expected.

With some trepidation I went down stairs and there in the middle of the hogsheads and barrels of beer was young Billy attempting to turn on their taps. Fortunately they were a bit too tight for him to move. I asked him what he was doing and he said that he wanted to know what was in 'the big wooden barrels'. I told him they were full of beer and if he had managed to open one he would have been covered in the stuff. And both his mum and me would have been angry. And his Uncle Norman would also have been angry. Very angry.

With an angelic smile he said: 'Alright Uncle Wilf, I won't come down here anymore.'

When the family returned my father said that had he been staying at the pub much longer he would have demolished the garages anyway. My new (sic) car duly arrived, a 1950 Austin Eight and proudly I took my sisters out for a run in it.

Tommy, as usual, made a joke: 'As Shakespeare said – All's well that's ado about nothing.'

'Just a comedy of errors,' I said, 'a storm in a tempest.'

The move was coming up and there was plenty to be done. Valuers had to agree what the furniture and fittings were worth; the brewery needed to check on its property; staff had to be placated to make sure they stayed with us until the end and, as my mother never ceased to remind us, there were a million and one domestic jobs to sort out.

'It's all right for your father,' she would regale me. 'All he has to do is run the pub. I've got to arrange the removal, sort out the gas and electricity people, fix up new schools for the girls, stop the papers and the milk and everything else.'

I pointed out that stopping the papers was no great job and all I got in return was: 'You know what I mean Wilf.'

However, as it was school holidays much of the organisation fell on me. I it was who transported my mother to and from the Wordsworths' Inn to allow her to measure for curtains, agree with Mrs Green which bits of furniture and other knick-knacks would stay and which would go, arrange the redecoration of the private quarters and check out the area for food suppliers and the like – such things as newspapers and milk I thought, but dare not say so to my mother.

I also had my own move to arrange. I was looking forward to a new term and a new job as head of department. The extra money would cushion my loss of pub earnings and there would be less travelling as I had decided to reduce my visits to the pub. My new flat was ready; convenient for school and close to the Headingley rugby and cricket grounds. It was, of course, my mother who supervised everything. And she let everyone know about it.

'I've not only got our own removal to fix up but now our Wilf's decided to move as well and I've had him to sort out.'

I glanced at my father who gave me one of those knowing looks and we both decided that, like Oscar Wilde, we knew the precise, psychological moment when to say nothing.

The big day arrived quickly enough and my comment when we moved into the Coach and Four five years before that ten o'clock on a Monday morning seemed a daft time to take over a new pub must have rubbed off on my father. The move out was still mid morning but on a Tuesday and the new tenants had decided not to open the pub until the evening. The Lowe's new pub could wait until the following day.

But before the move my parents decided to throw a couple of parties. One was for the pub regulars, although we realised that when word got around we would have an enormous number of 'regulars'. The other would be for the staff and close friends.

The first party was on the final Sunday evening. Ronnie Taylor, our resident pianist, provided the entertainment along with George Rimmer, a local comedian, a bit past his best but very popular and just the man for such an occasion. My mother and the girls laid on a magnificent buffet and father decided to sell all drinks at half price for the first hour.

They were queuing by half past six. We liked to think the success of the evening was due to the popularity of the Lowe family but there was a suspicion that the free food and cheap booze may have had something to do with it. Nevertheless, it was a great evening despite seeing some of our 'regulars' for the first time. My father endeared himself by thanking his many regulars – both regular and not so regular – for their custom over the past five years and then offering half price drinks again for the first hour in his new pub in three days time.

The Smithies had organised a collection which was enlarged

during the evening as Bob and Eric along with Norman sought out the 'not so regulars' and shamed them into subscribing. Father got a stand season ticket for the Calderthorpe rugby league matches and my mother was given a voucher for one of the top stores in Leeds and a bunch of flowers. The girls got book vouchers and even I was presented with a dozen golf balls.

The following night was for the private affair and invitations were strictly limited. I was given the hard word by my mother: 'None of you asking your mates along just because they've bought you a drink or two,' she said. In the event it was my mother who overstepped the limit. Among the forty or so guests who were asked to stay behind after time was called on that final night were her hairdresser, the landlady of a pub in Calderthorpe who she hadn't seen for three years but who happened to phone her up on that day to wish her well, and the bank manager who made his first ever visit to the Coach and Four.

The police had been informed. This was a private party; no money would change hands, it would be well behaved – father hoped! – and, in any case, two members of the force and a magistrate had been invited. Other guests included a clutch of the town's licensees, our closest friends, relatives who could make it and, of course, the hard working staff. Plus my mother's separate list.

It was a quiet evening and Norman had the pub emptied and the front door bolted well before normal closing time. His valedictory tone that we needed to pack before tomorrow morning's departure saw folk off without trouble but with many farewells. As it was the packing was all done and most of the furniture had left and was spending the next two nights in the removal company's depository. The family wanted an easy morning.

Ronnie Taylor was tickling the ivories, as he chose to call it, and an assortment of landladies were laying out a buffet prepared by them as a present to my mother. The old man had invested in a case of champagne and the brewery had sent along a couple of cases of its special celebratory ale, a beer brewed once a year, used for special occasions and never put on public sale. It had all the makings of a great evening.

And so it was and this time it was the family's turn to make the presentations. To Norman, Vera, Mary, to our two regular waiters and the two cleaners; to Jack Thornton, the brewery's area manager, and, much to everyone's surprise and delight, to Sergeant Bert Powell. He was the man, my father said, who as everybody knew, ran the Oldford police division – never mind the Inspectors and Superintendents. He went on to parody W S Gilbert by saying: 'When constabulary duty's to be done, a policeman's lot is quite a happy one.'

Bert responded by wishing the old man well in his new pub and saying: 'Always open on time Alex, and the rest will take care of itself.'

There was a very obvious omission from the presentations although Brian Dyson didn't look too concerned at being overlooked. Then my father explained: 'You may have noticed that there was nothing for Brian. I had intended offering him a free pint a day for a year but I thought it would be less expensive to offer him a job instead. I'm delighted to tell you that Brian is to become my manager, bar cellarman, car park attendant, relief cleaner, Poo Bah and Lord High Everything Else, as my old mate W S Gilbert might have put it.'

It had been a well kept secret between my folks and Brian. Even Norman was out of the picture and he reckoned that nothing went on in Oldford without him being aware of it. Brian was to live in the flat attached to the pub and regarded the job as an ideal opportunity to groom himself for a move to his own pub.

There was just one more short speech from Alderman Alfie Hetherington, twice Mayor of Oldford, but present that evening in his capacity as a close friend and a pub regular. He merely thanked the family for running a fine pub and being good friends and company. He wished them well in the new pub and quoted some half-remembered bit of Gilbert that: 'It isn't so much what's on the table that matters, as what's on the chairs.'

The rest of the evening passed in a somewhat sentimental mood with promises of keeping in touch and regularly visiting one another. The following night the family was to stay at the Royal George Hotel ready for an early start at the Wordsworths' Inn. So the final session with the Lowe family in control at the Coach and Four at Oldford in the West Riding of Yorkshire drew slowly to a close.

'One for the road,' said Alfie Hetherington.

'Time gentlemen, and ladies, please!' called Bert Powell.

'It's my round,' said my father.

'Quite right,' said my mother, who always had the last word.

Moving on from The Coach

JOIN CAMRA

If you like good beer and good pubs you could be helping to fight to preserve, protect and promote them. CAMRA was set up in the early Seventies to fight against the mass destruction of a part of Britain's heritage. The giant brewers are still pushing through takeovers, mergers and closures of their smaller regional rivals. They are still trying to impose national brands of beer and lager on their customers whether they like it or not, and they are still closing down town and village pubs or converting them into grotesque 'theme' pubs.

CAMRA wants to see genuine free competition in the brewing industry, fair prices, and, above all, a top quality product brewed by local breweries in accordance with local tastes, and served in pubs that maintain the best features of a tradition that goes back centuries. As a CAMRA member you will be able to enjoy generous discounts on CAMRA products and receive the highly rated monthly newspaper *What's Brewing*. You will be given the CAMRA members' handbook and be able to join in local social events and brewery trips. To join, complete the form below and, if you wish, arrange for direct debit payments by filling in the form overleaf and returning it to CAMRA. To pay by credit card, contact the membership secretary on (01727) 867201.

Full single UK/EU £16; Joint (living partners) UK/EU £19; Single under 26, Student, Disabled, Unemployed, Retired over 60 £9; Joint retired over 60, Joint under 26 £12; UK/EU Life £192, UK/EU Joint life £228. Single life retired over 60 £90, Joint life retired over 60 £120. Full overseas membership £20, Joint overseas membership £23. Single overseas life £240, Joint overseas life £276.

Please delete as appropriate:

I/We wish to become members of CAMRA.

I/We agree to abide by the memorandum and articles of association of the company.

I/We enclose a cheque/p. o. for £   (payable to CAMRA Ltd.)

Name(s)

Address

Postcode

Signature(s)

CAMRA Ltd. , 230 Hatfield Road, St Albans, Herts AL1 4LW

Please fill in the whole form using a ball point pen and send it to:

Instruction to your Bank or Building Society to pay by Direct Debit

Campaign for Real Ale Ltd,
230 Hatfield Road,
St. Albans,
Herts
AL1 4LW

Originator's Identification Number

| 9 | 2 | 6 | 1 | 2 | 9 |

Reference Number

| | | | | | | | | | | | | | | |

Name of Account Holder(s)

FOR CAMRA OFFICIAL USE ONLY

This is not part of the instruction to your Bank or Building Society

Membership Number

Name

Postcode

Bank/Building Society account number

| | | | | | | | |

Branch Sort Code

| | | | | | |

Name and full postal address of your Bank or Building Society

| To The Manager | Bank/Building Society |

Address

Postcode

Instructions to your Bank or Building Society
Please pay CAMRA Direct Debits from the account detailed on this instruction subject to the safeguards assured by the Direct Debit Guarantee. I understand that this instruction may remain with CAMRA and, if so, will be passed electronically to my Bank/Building Society

Signature(s)

Date

Banks and Building Societies may not accept Direct Debit instructions for some types of account

---- ✂ -

This guarantee should be detached and retained by the Payer.

The Direct Debit Guarantee

■ This Guarantee is offered by all Banks and Building Societies that take part in the Direct Debit Scheme. The efficiency and security of the Scheme is monitored and protected by your own Bank or Building Society.

■ If the amounts to be paid or the payment dates change CAMRA will notify you 10 working days in advance of your account being debited or as otherwise agreed.

■ If an error is made by CAMRA or your Bank or Building Society, you are guaranteed a full and immediate refund from your branch of the amount paid.

■ You can cancel a Direct Debit at any time by writing to your Bank or Building Society. Please also send a copy of your letter to us.

CAMRA BOOKS

The CAMRA Books range of guides helps you search out the best in beer (and cider) and brew it at home too!

Buying in the UK

All our books are available through bookshops in the UK. If you can't find a book, simply order it from your bookshop using the ISBN number, title and author details given below. CAMRA members should refer to their regular monthly newspaper What's Brewing for the latest details and member special offers. CAMRA books are also available by mail-order (postage free in UK) from: CAMRA Books, 230 Hatfield Road, St Albans, Herts, AL1 4LW. Cheques made payable to CAMRA Ltd. Telephone your credit card order on 01727 867201.

Buying outside the UK

CAMRA books are also sold in many book and beer outlets in the USA and other English-speaking countries. If you have trouble locating a particular book, use the details below to order with your credit card (or US$ cheque) by mail, email (info@camra. org. uk), fax (+44 1727 867670) or web site. The web site (www. camra. org. uk) will securely process credit card purchases.

Carriage of £2.00 per book (Europe) and £3.00 per book (US, Australia, New Zealand and other overseas) is charged.

UK Booksellers

Call CAMRA Books for distribution details and book list. CAMRA Books are listed on all major CD-ROM book lists and on our Internet site: http://www. camra. org. uk

Overseas Booksellers

Call or fax CAMRA Books for details of local distributors.

Distributors are required for some English language territories and rights are available for electronic and non-English language editions. Enquiries should be addressed to the managing editor (mark-webb@msn. com).

Good Bottled Beer Guide

By Jeff Evans   224 pages   Price: £8.99

The definitive guide to real ale in a bottle:

- all UK breweries which produce bottle-conditioned beer
- tasting notes to help you choose carefully
- the background to each beer
- where the beer is on sale
- key dates in bottled beer history
- how to buy, keep and serve bottled real ale
- the best foreign bottle-conditioned beers

Highly commended by the British Guild of Beer Writers, this book has the answers for those who like the idea of trying some of the most creatively brewed beers in the world. There are more than 300 to choose from, all from the comfort of your armchair!

Use the following code to order this book from your bookshop:
ISBN   1-85249-173-6

Real Ale Almanac

By Roger Protz   320 pages   Price: £8.99

The Almanac is unique among beer books in listing every cask-conditioned beer brewed in Britain. This new edition lists brewpubs as well as commercial breweries. The Almanac also gives full details of the ingredients used for each beer – malts and hops in particular – along with author Roger Protz's own tasting notes based on a quarter-century experience of the brewing industry. The Almanac also indicates which beers are organic and those which are suitable for vegetarians and vegans.

Use the following code to order this book from your bookshop:
ISBN   1-85249-170-1

India Pale Ale (Homebrew Classics series)

by Clive La Pensée and Roger Protz

Pages: 196 pages   Price: £8.99

Beer journalist Roger Protz goes on an historical hunt for the origins of what is perhaps the most famous beer of all time – IPA. He uncovers the whereabouts of the original brewery where IPA was devised as an export for the colonies, an invention that made its brewers extremely wealthy men.

Brewer La Pensée conjures up the smells and sounds of breweries and brewers spanning three centuries, all brewing their version of IPA.

Use the following code to order this book from your bookshop:
ISBN: 1-85249-129-9

CAMRA's London Pubs Guide

by Lynne Pearce   224 pages   **Price: £9.99**

This is the guide to CAMRA's favourite London pubs, chosen because these pubs sell traditional real ale, often brewed in the capital itself. The guide also points out the pub features you will want to discover on your trip around London: the architecture, personalities, history, local ambience and nearby attractions.

Practical aids to getting you to the pub(s) of your choice include transportation details and street level maps. Each entry also provides information about opening times, travel details, food arrangements, parking, disabled and children's facilities. Plus the all-important range of beers.

Feature articles in the book include a history of brewing in London and a guide to London's best pub food. Real ale and great food in London pubs with stories to tell. What could be better?

Use the following code to order this book from your bookshop:
ISBN 1-85249-164-7

CAMRA's Good Cider Guide

by David Matthews   400 pages   **Price: £9.99**

CAMRA's guide to real cider researched anew for the new Millennium and now with features on cider around the world. The guide contains features on cider-making, a comprehensive and detailed guide to UK producers of cider and a brand new listing of outlets – pubs, restaurants, bars, small cider makers – with full address including postcode and telephone contact numbers. Also provided are details of ciders available and, where appropriate, items of interest in the pub or area.

Use the following code to order this book from your bookshop:
ISBN 1-85249-143-4

Dictionary of Beer

By CAMRA   208 pages   Price: £7.99

A unique reference work. Where else would you find definitions of the following words grouped together: parachute, Paradise, paraflow and paralytic? Or skull-dragged, slummage and snob screen? More than 2000 detailed definitions. This dictionary covers brewing techniques and ingredients; international beers and breweries; tasting (beer evaluation) terms; historical references and organisations; British real ale breweries; slang phrases and abbreviations; culinary terms and beer cocktails; and much more.

Use the following code to order this book from your bookshop:
ISBN   1-85249-158-2

50 Great Pub Crawls

by Barrie Pepper   256 pages   Price: £9.99

Visit the beer trails of the UK, from town centre walks, to hikes and bikes and a crawl on a train on which the pubs are even situated on your side of the track! Barrie Pepper, with contributions and recommendations from CAMRA branches, has compiled a 'must do' list of pub crawls, with easy to use colour maps to guide you, notes on architecture, history and brewing tradition to entertain you.

Use the following code to order this book from your bookshop:
ISBN 1-85249-142-6

Brew Your Own British Real Ale at Home

by Graham Wheeler and Roger Protz

194 pages   Price: £8.99

This book contains recipes which allow you to replicate some famous cask-conditioned beers at home or to customise brews to your own particular taste. Conversion details are given so that the measurements can be used world-wide.

Use the following code to order this book from your bookshop:
ISBN 1-85249-138-8

Brew Classic European Beers at Home

by Graham Wheeler and Roger Protz

196 pages   Price: £8.99

Keen home brewers can now recreate some of the world's classic beers. In your own home you can brew superb pale ales, milds, porters, stouts, Pilsners, Alt, Kolsch, Trappist, wheat beers, sour beers, even the astonishing fruit lambics of Belgium… and many more. Measurements are given in UK, US and European units, emphasising the truly international scope of the beer styles within.

Use the following code to order this book from your bookshop: ISBN 1-85249-117-5

Home Brewing

by Graham Wheeler   240 pages   Price: £8.99

Recently redesigned to make it even easier to use, this is the classic first book for all home-brewers. While being truly comprehensive, Home Brewing also manages to be a practical guide which can be followed step by step as you try your first brews. Plenty of recipes for beginners and hints and tips from the world's most revered home brewer.

Use the following code to order this book from your bookshop: ISBN 1-85249-137-X

Heritage Pubs of Great Britain

by Mark Bolton and James Belsey

144 pages hard back   Price: £16.99

It is still possible to enjoy real ale in sight of great craftsmanship and skill. Feast your eyes and toast the architects and builders from times past. This full-colour 'coffee-table' production is a photographic record of some of the finest pub interiors in Britain. As a collector's item, it is presented on heavy, gloss-art paper in a sleeved hard-back format.

The pub interiors have been photographed by architectural specialist Mark Bolton and described in words by pub expert James Belsey.

Available only directly from CAMRA – call 01727 867201

(overseas +44 1727 867201)